AN AVALON HISTORICAL ROMANCE

THE HONORABLE MARKSLEY

Sherry Lynn Ferguson

Richard Marksley, home from the Peninsular War, is used to correcting the errors and excesses of his aristocratic relations. But this time his dissolute cousin Reginald, the Viscount Langsford, has truly gone too far. Posing as Richard, Reggie has compromised the reputation of a young gentlewoman and left Richard to right the situation.

Richard would much rather be pursuing poets for his publication, *The Tantalus*. But his sense of responsibility and family honor make it impossible for him to turn his back on the situation, and he's determined to find a remedy—short of actually marrying the girl!

Hallie Ashton has limited choice. Her uncle is convinced that she has gone astray, and with Richard, not the truant Reggie. With her family pressing for a wedding, Hallie faces the demands of proper society that threaten to steal her future and seal her fate. If she could explain the situation to Marksley herself, she might find him to be a useful ally. But that would require revealing the secret closest to her heart.

THE HONORABLE MARKSLEY

•

Sherry Lynn Ferguson

AVALON BOOKS
NEW YORK

Fe

Chapter One

Neither the Earl of Penham nor his son Reginald, the Viscount Langsford, had ever shown the slightest interest in the source of the family's wealth, though they were mightily beholden to its continuance.

Richard Marksley mused on that as he drew his horse to a halt and surveyed with pride the extensive pastures behind Penham Hall. Pride was all he could claim for his hard work, since Penham was not, and never would be, his. The privilege of possession lay solely with his uncle and his reprobate of a cousin. But Richard had been Penham's responsible keeper for many years, and the estate exhibited his care.

"You must be pleased, sir," Appleby said. The steward had drawn his own horse even with Richard's Apollo. "The old place looks much better than you had hoped."

"Indeed," Richard said. On this particularly fine

September morning, with the light strengthening over the dew-damp grass, Penham looked peaceful and prosperous. "'Tis difficult to credit that Reginald as good as gambled the place away this summer."

"I doubt the Viscount would ever do so intentionally, sir."

Richard spared him a smile. "You are unfailingly kind, Appleby. For that, and your good sense, I am always grateful."

"I thank you, sir."

"We will do well enough this year," Richard observed, looking back at the Hall, "but the future must be addressed. Penham must grow if it is to survive. The estate cannot merely be preserved." The word might as easily have comprehended his invalid of an uncle. At the impending prospect of Reginald as Earl, Richard felt a distinct chill.

He had ridden out early and hard. Now he turned Apollo toward home.

"This tour has been helpful, Appleby. We meet again at Ludlow's, Thursday next?" When the steward nodded, Richard urged Apollo to a canter and headed back to Archers, the small but comfortable manor that had come to him ten years before—on his twentieth birthday. Again he blessed the fact that the property shared only one boundary with Penham. By road, the distance was four miles; across the fields and fences it was scarcely one. The greater the remove from his family the better, particularly at a time like this, when his patience was at ebb.

He scarcely noticed the magnificent beeches framing Archers's warm brick. Instead he strode directly across the stable yard to his library, determined to pen a few additional instructions for Appleby. The steward, he reflected, was a competent and genial man whose only fault was a forgiving memory. He continually underestimated the Viscount Langsford's extravagance.

Richard no longer made the same mistake. Reggie's behavior, summer after summer, had predictably rivaled that of every preceding summer, and this season's reckonings were another abomination.

The debts tallied to embarrassing sums. Worthier endeavors would suffer in order to keep Reggie flush with funds. Richard considered it a testament to his own ingenuity, and to Appleby's management, that they had devised rescues time and again. But he feared for the future. There were too many pressing demands upon the estate and its resources to let Reggie's escapades continue unchecked.

Reggie, he decided, could not have planned a more exasperating birthday gift.

Gibbs had been waiting quietly just outside the library doors. As the butler coughed gently, Richard rose to give him a few items for the morning's post.

"You are too patient, Gibbs," he said, handing the papers to the older man. "You should have coughed earlier."

"Not at all, sir," Gibbs protested, "I had no thought to interrupt you. But this has just come by messenger.

And you have always said, that whenever such as these should come—"

Richard snatched the thin letter from Gibbs's hand and quickly scanned the familiar scrawl: "I had promised you a poem, but unexpected demands have made it difficult for me to finish . . . little time for application . . . do apologize . . ." Richard's lips thinned as he read. So the anticipated work from Henry Beecham would not be available for next month's issue of *The Tantalus*. He should have known the elusive man would eventually disappoint him in this way as well; most of the journal's contributors had found reason on one occasion or another to disoblige their publisher. He had assumed, unreasonably, that Beecham would be different.

"And the messenger?" he asked, at last looking at Gibbs. "Is he outside?"

"Already on his way, sir. I could not keep him. Not even with the gift of a crown. He did say he had come directly from a rider in Guildford."

"And that rider no doubt from yet another obscure little village." Richard sighed. "It seems Mr. Beecham truly has no desire to be known to us, Gibbs. And October's *Tantalus* will lack a new poem."

"I am sorry, sir. 'Tis a fine journal."

"Thank you, Gibbs." Richard smiled, aware that his butler preferred the racing results from Epsom. "You do much for the cause." But Gibbs was shifting impatiently in front of him. "Is there something else?"

"Yes, sir. In the drawing room. The countess is here, sir. Lady Penham."

"At this hour? No wonder you look so pale." Richard turned to his library and crowded desk. "You'd best show her in here, then. She will excuse herself all the more readily from any evidence of actual labor."

"Yes, sir. I mean, very good, sir." As Gibbs departed Richard glanced reluctantly at his work. The papers now awaiting his attention concerned his chosen avocation, his one passion—the production of a bimonthly literary and opinion journal. Over the past two years, *The Tantalus* had drawn public and critical acclaim, delighting both its sponsors and its contributors. Richard quite naturally believed any commendation was deserved. With organization and application, and the means he could spare, he had given talents like Henry Beecham a forum.

That particular poet, he considered grimly, had no reason to be coy.

Only a year ago he had received the first Beecham poems, a trio of such quiet strength and appeal that Richard had been captivated. He believed them to be the work of an established wordsmith of his acquaintance, someone among the literary set in London. Yet inquiries had revealed no clue to the man's identity or whereabouts. Subsequent poems found their way to him via baffling routings of messengers and postings, much like this morning's missive. It seemed Henry

Beecham enjoyed puzzles. And now, perhaps, he no longer even cared to be read.

On *The Tantalus*'s accounts a tidy sum accumulated, unclaimed, in Beecham's name.

"Cheeky scop," Richard muttered softly, "haven't you need of the lucre?"

"I do not care for your tone, Richard," his aunt said sharply from behind him, compelling him to turn. "'Tis most abusive. With whom do you imagine yourself at odds?"

"With myself, madam," Richard acknowledged with a bow. Geneve Marksley, the Countess of Penham, was, as always, fashionably dressed, in a pink morning gown that flattered the artificial blooms in her cheeks. Her hair was still gold, her azure eyes still bright, but Richard had long ago discovered their blindness to anything beyond clothes, society, and her darling Reginald.

When she offered her hand, he took it and bowed low, but he did not kiss her. Geneve and the Earl had raised him from the age of twelve, when he had lost his parents, and in all that time he had learned to respond in kind.

"Dear Richard, I am so gratified to find you home. You spend so much time away with your . . . hobbies." She glanced dismissively at his crowded desk. "We really must speak."

As the two comfortable chairs by the fire were temporarily hosting parcels of books, Richard offered her his own desk chair and chose to remain standing. Anything, he thought, to speed the visit.

"How well you look," Geneve said as she settled her skirts. To her credit she might actually have looked at him, but Richard only acknowledged the compliment with the slightest tilt of his head. Geneve rarely spoke to him without considering her direction. And he knew this was no birthday call.

"I fear our Reginald has done something rather dreadful." Her indulgent smile robbed the words of any reprimand.

Richard stifled his instant distaste for the inclusive "our."

"I must agree with you, madam. Unless, of course, you refer to something other than his obscene debts?"

"His debts? Really, Richard, why should I know anything of the sort? Reginald should not be living like a pauper. You and his father are supposed to arrange for him to have what he ought." Richard's lips firmed. "No, my dear. This is truly serious. I cannot imagine. . . . Well, the damage has been done. And she is really quite attractive, though not at all the sort one would choose for our Reginald, of course. Which is why I thought of you at once, and not only because of the name, mind you. It is, to be quite honest, your problem now, and not dear Reginald's—"

"If you please, ma'am," Richard interrupted, "I fail to understand you."

"Ah! Well—it seems we must believe Reginald has compromised a girl. A most impressionable young woman, to be sure, but a gently-bred miss, nonetheless. Her uncle is being frightfully tiresome."

Richard looked through the tall French doors and out at the courtyard garden. This was not the first time Reggie had pursued the temptation of a pretty face. Could his cousin never exercise any judgment? Despite a ready supply of willing muslin, he persistently ignored the strictures, though to date he had not strayed into the more carefully tended folds of the eligible.

When Richard's attention returned to his aunt, he realized why mannerly behavior was so rare in his cousin. Excuses flowed as bountifully as her devotion.

"How much does this offended personage want?" he asked wearily.

Geneve shrugged. "My dear Richard, if it were only that, I should scarcely have had to trouble you this morning. No, this particular gentleman, this Alfred Ashton, is most insistent on a wedding. He is . . . beside himself, and has even spoken of a special license."

Richard barely restrained a smile. It seemed that dear Reginald had finally been snared. But Geneve was not smiling.

"You needn't look so superior, Richard, as this concerns you as well."

"In what way, madam?"

"Apparently Reginald used your name."

"Used it?"

"The Ashtons believe the Viscount Langsford is Richard Marksley. 'Tis R.E. Marksley, Richard *Evan* Marksley, they intend to bring to heel, and not my son, Reginald Falsworth."

Richard's hands tightened into fists. "Where is Reggie now?"

"Reginald? Why, he left for Ireland yesterday."

"And my *dear* cousin told you that he used my name? Why would you not simply acquaint these people with the truth?" His anger summoned a stubborn line to Geneve's lips.

"Reginald left me a note with an apology."

"How considerate of him to apologize to his mother. Although—if I understand you—at least three other people are more deserving of that courtesy."

"You are too sharp, Richard. You always have been. And how was I to tell the Ashtons the truth? Think what that would mean for Reginald!"

"Believe me, I am quite aware of what it might mean for him."

"You have never understood the responsibility he faces as Cyril's heir. All the demands of position, no small matters I assure you, scarcely balance the benefits you are so fond of pointing out to him. In fact, I have wondered if you might even resent him." As she surveyed her smoothly-gloved fingers, Richard schooled his features. He had heard the charge on more than one occasion; its injustice no longer rankled. He had determined long ago that he would much rather be the gentleman he was than Reginald Falsworth Marksley.

"In any case, madam, why are you here?"

Geneve looked astonished. "I have already told you. You must marry the girl. Or at least set to rights the family's standing. This mustn't be bruited about. Permit Ashton to have the banns published, or some such. Perhaps you shall be clever enough to stop a marriage. I know you can be terribly clever, Richard, with your head for figures and your little journal."

"You would *endorse* my substitution for Reggie?"

"Why, I believe it most necessary. You are, after all, R.E. Marksley. And you are his cousin."

"But I am not *the man*, madam. Hardly a minor consideration. Ashton's niece must have found something appealing in Reggie. Or, should I say, in his behavior."

Geneve had not listened. She fingered her skirts and added proudly, "Reginald has more than a title to recommend him, as you well know. He is such a handsome, good-natured young man. 'Tis no surprise to me that the ladies are quite wild for him."

"You wisely use the plural, madam. This is not the first time Reggie has made promises to females, promises he had no intention of keeping. Unfortunately, he has only one cousin whom he can leg-shackle. What would you propose he do with the next adoring damsel?"

"You've no call to be impertinent, Richard. When I come to you for help, I should expect more. But you can only criticize—" She probed her reticule for a linen square. "We have asked nothing of you. Nothing—after all we have done for you. This is your cousin, your only cousin, who has been like a brother to you. How can you turn your back on him?"

She managed to squeeze a single tear from her beseeching eyes. Richard watched her with little tolerance and less feeling. Reggie had been sly, spoiled, and cruel all his life. It was true that he and Richard were of an age, but far from brothers.

"I have one suggestion, my dear aunt. And that is that you and Mr. Ashton await Reggie's return from Ireland. Let him explain himself to the girl. Perhaps she still believes he is fond of her. Once disabused of that notion, no rational being would have him."

"But you simply do not understand. Reginald compromised Miss Ashton. They were alone together, they were seen. Her wishes are of no consequence. No consequence at all. Her uncle insists on a wedding."

Richard stared accusingly at his aunt. "The young lady's virtue. . .?"

"Is unquestioned! Really, Richard, 'tis indelicate of you even to ask. Reginald is your cousin, and a gentleman." She avoided his gaze. "You must not draw such conclusions, merely because this has happened so precipitously. Just before Reginald left."

"I am certain his departure was just as precipitous."

Geneve sat very straight. "He wrote that his plans for Ireland were made months ago. 'Tis beneath you to imply that he would so deceive us."

"As he has certainly deceived the Ashtons?" As Geneve started to pout, Richard pressed her. "When does he intend to return?"

"In two months."

"Two *months*?" Abruptly, Richard paced, moving to the garden doors and moodily staring out at the small courtyard. The morning sun was beginning to warm the gravel walk. A few roses lingered in the autumn air. They seemed to mock his confinement. He knew he would have to deal with this as he had dealt with everything else. Yet still it infuriated him.

Reggie would have thought it all a grand joke—to pose as his cousin, then flee the country. He must be having a good laugh just now. And Richard hoped Reggie choked on whatever expensive Madeira he was no doubt at that moment imbibing.

"Richard . . . Richard." His aunt's voice behind him was softer than he had ever heard it. "If he were not my son I would never ask it of you. But now I must beg you. How can he—who will be an Earl, who will inherit Penham and so much more—marry a simple country girl, a vicar's daughter? 'Twould be ruin for everything we ever hoped for him. He is our only son, Richard. We must think of the family. Of the Marksley name. If you do this for us now, I shall never ask anything of you again. I do promise you."

Richard closed his eyes. Part of him wondered what Reggie—the Gorgeous Langsford, as the *ton*'s wags had christened him—had ever done to deserve such love. Certainly he himself had received no portion of it, though as a boy he had tried often enough to earn some. Still, it was folly to question any mother's affections, even as frivolously distracted and careless a mother as

Geneve. What had to interest him now was her promise. To have nothing ever asked of him again. What a relief that must be!

He turned to face her. She had risen from her seat and now stood toying with her kerchief.

"Is the family that objectionable?"

"They are respectable enough, I suppose. Mr. Ashton has considerable property in Berkshire, where the family has an acceptable history. The home is included on the local tours in Tewsbury, as the cousin—a Miss Binkin—would have me believe. The girl, Miss Ashton, is his brother's only child. I gather Ashton lost his own son on the Continent, which no doubt concerns him greatly in this."

"Do you suspect this was arranged, to set her cap for a lord? To elevate the family's prospects by trapping just such a one as Reggie?"

"I cannot believe it, Richard. But she's a quiet enough young woman. Perhaps the . . . the passions of the moment simply overwhelmed her."

Or more likely Reggie's passions did, Richard added silently. Any woman so enamored of his cousin could only find true feeling foreign. Doubtless Miss Ashton was a silly chit of limited sensitivity and even less intelligence. It would take some doing to convince such a creature that any decently responsible young farmer would make her a better husband.

"I'll go see this . . . charmer. And her ambitious uncle. 'Twill be a day before I can leave for Berkshire and another day to reach them. With luck we will come to some understanding on Friday. I have every intention of convincing them to find a husband elsewhere. With Penham's support, of course." He bowed, but his aunt was no longer meeting his gaze.

"Richard, they have come to us. And I . . . I have brought the Ashtons here. To Archers. The Ashtons and the cousin, Miss Binkin. Gibbs was to see them into the drawing room."

The trespass heightened the offense. Richard must have looked his accusation.

"Alfred Ashton insisted," his aunt complained. "What was I to do?"

"He does sound a most pleasant, accommodating gentleman. Well then, I shall speak to them at once."

"Richard! But you cannot address them so!" She was genuinely distressed. He had forgotten that he still wore his riding clothes and soiled boots, that he had loosened his cravat. His face was still unshaven. But that was certainly not exceptional so early in the morning and in one's own home. As he buttoned his coat he reminded himself that he had not yet had breakfast.

"I admit I have been rushed, madam, but I believe I am presentable for all that. It seems best to move with dispatch. The Ashtons have been waiting this half hour. I intend to spare them any further affront."

"It is undignified, Richard," Geneve said reprovingly, "in all your dirt—to look as though you are just come from the stables!"

"As I am, dear aunt. But I believe you made me a promise. And in any event, if this Miss Ashton thinks to make me a husband," he neatly and abruptly tightened the linen at his neck, "she shall see me much worse." And with that he turned to the door.

Chapter Two

Hallie, gazing out at the garden, scarcely heard her uncle's grumbling. He was once again airing his displeasure with the Countess of Penham and her son, the Viscount. Cousin Millicent sat silently at attention, occasionally nodding agreement. But Hallie, too conscious of the bright morning and the sweet twitter of birds in the shrubbery, could only listen with impatience. For the past two days, her uncle's constant complaints had ruled all conversation.

Had she been able to credit him with a relative's sincere concern for the welfare of a niece, or for any young woman's straitened circumstances, she might have drawn some slight solace from his temper. But that she could not do. She knew he was uncomfortable and embarrassed and that he blamed her for making him feel so. Her offense, to him and to decent society, had been great, very great indeed. His one aim for his stubborn charge had been to provide well for her through marriage. If she now netted a lord, the union would be a hushed affair, less than the notable event that might have soothed him. But Alfred Ashton would see to it that the lord was caught. He continued to insist upon that conclusion to this shameful situation, though the prospect repelled her.

Her uncle had no knowledge of the precise infraction of which she and Marksley were guilty, but upon his return three days ago, he had found his cousin, Hallie's unwelcome companion, convinced of her charge's irredeemable, public disgrace. If Millicent and her extensive network of gossips had determined such to be the case, Hallie could not dispute it. It was true that Marksley had kissed her; she wished he had not. It was true that Millicent had surprised them in an embrace; Hallie had invited neither the embrace nor its subsequent broadcast. Within one minute of meeting Marksley, Hallie had known he was not the kind of man who would improve on further acquaintance. Yet courtesy had demanded that she listen when he drew her aside—surely she had owed him that—and he had taken advantage of their brief moment alone. For her indulgence she would pay dearly.

As she heard the drawing room doors open behind her, the grumbles from her uncle ceased. Even before Hallie turned, she sensed his continuing glower. Yet when she did turn she started. Her uncle had no cause for objection, no reason to seethe, for this was not the man they sought.

A dark gaze returned her own. For a second she felt relief. Then a dreadful premonition shortened her breath.

"Mr. Ashton," the newcomer said, his gaze moving to her uncle as he bowed, "I am Richard Marksley."

She thought her uncle would pop.

"I know very well who you are, *sir*," he snapped. "You should have done me the honor of speaking to me before this."

Again that assessing gaze met hers. She knew she had suffered a shock. All her expectations for this meeting had been based on error; she had to protest. Yet she was too overwhelmingly glad that Richard Marksley was not the man she had thought him to be.

"My apologies, sir," he said now. "You understand my hesitance. My . . . welcome was by no means assured."

"Welcome indeed, you . . . blackguard! What the devil do you mean with my girl?"

"He means to marry her, sir," the Countess supplied. She had entered behind Marksley, but her glance at him was less confident than her tone.

"Oh that he will, milady," her uncle grated, "and before the month is out."

Hallie could not credit it, that Richard Marksley would claim to have compromised a woman he had never even met. As he moved further into the room, toward her, Hallie studied him. He did not *look* mad.

Taller than the average, with rich brown hair and strong, somewhat severe features, Richard Marksley struck her as a man who would be at ease in any circle. Yet his character was less transparent than that of his imitator.

Again she sought those arresting eyes. She could not judge their color, only their effect.

"Before you commit yourself, sir, and your niece," this time he bowed slightly toward Hallie, "I should inform you that I am not in fact the Viscount Langsford, as you may have been led to believe."

"Not the . . . then who in blazes are you?"

"Richard Evan Marksley, sir. R.E. Marksley. Nephew to the Earl of Penham and his countess, Lady Penham. First cousin of Reginald Falsworth Marksley, the Viscount Langsford." He repeated his restrained bow, then looked directly at Hallie. This time she thought his gaze a challenge.

"All very well and good, young man. But to the point—you have insulted my family. You compromised my niece. If you were a smithy or a peddler, you'd still be lending her your name."

One of Richard Marksley's fine eyebrows rose. "You would consign her to such a fate?"

"I'll not have her dishonored."

"You and I, sir, might debate the meaning of honor." Marksley's voice hinted at a degree of warmth. "But I perceive you are in a hurry."

"That I am, Marksley," her uncle said roughly. "To see you wed."

"Uncle," Hallie said, aware that Marksley was

instantly alert to her voice. "This gentleman just told you that he is not the Viscount Langsford. He is not—"

"This gentleman? Bah! Defend him, would you?"

Even faced with her uncle's bluster, Hallie was conscious of Marksley's attention.

"No doubt Miss Ashton wishes you to reconsider the matter," he said, "as you have only one niece—and I clearly am not the lord you had been led to expect."

"Deceitful devil! You, sir, sully your family's name."

At the charge, something about Marksley at once seemed dangerous, though Hallie could not have explained what in him had changed. Certainly the stiff set of his shoulders had not varied.

"Yet you would still see me lend that name to yours?" he asked coldly.

"Aye, that I would. That I *will*."

"Gentlemen," the Countess said. "This is most unseemly. I would suggest you move on to resolving this matter. Surely Miss Ashton can only prefer to prevent a quarrel." She turned a practiced smile on Hallie, a smile that was not returned. That the Countess would shield her own unmannerly son at the expense of another filled Hallie with contempt.

"Uncle," she said again, though her throat was dry, "I have no wish to marry this gentleman."

"Hoity-toity, miss," he mocked. "You might have thought of that before closeting yourself with him. What you wish don't signify."

Even as Hallie swallowed her anger, she caught Marksley examining her stubborn face.

"Perhaps Miss Ashton still hopes for a more advantageous match," he suggested, and the positive impression Hallie had formed of him fled.

"Watch what you say, Marksley," her uncle growled. "The girl will be your wife. I shan't have her abused."

"That is a privilege you reserve to yourself then, sir?"

"Richard!" The countess glided swiftly between the two. "This will not do. Of course you are . . . you are resigned to your duty, though it is not perhaps to your liking. All of us must simply make the best of this deplorable situation. You owe Miss Ashton an apology."

Marksley looked from her uncle to Hallie. "I apologize, Miss Ashton, for not being my cousin."

Hallie met his chilly gaze and wondered if that were the source of his scorn. He thought she craved a title or that she had lost her heart to his knavish relative. His most ungracious act was to believe her so insensible.

"Harriet Ashton," her uncle demanded, "what do you say to the man?" Yet she could think of nothing to say to him. Not a word to R.E. Marksley. The irony of that left her mute.

"Perhaps," Marksley offered, "Miss Ashton and I might have a moment alone?"

His aunt objected.

" 'Twould be most improper, Richard. Miss Binkin must accompany you."

"Surely, my lady, we are beyond requiring a chaperone? Although we have not, as you know," Marksley turned to her uncle, "had much time together."

"Too bloody much, if you ask me," he fumed as Marksley moved to the door. "But there ain't much more you can trespass against now, is there?"

At so great an insult, Hallie expected the two men to come to blows. But with a slight bow and the sweep of one arm Marksley motioned Hallie to precede him.

She brushed past him quickly, aware as she did so that he was taller than his cousin—her eyes were on a level with his shoulders. And at close quarters the strength of his restraint was palpable. He could only disdain her entire family.

In the hall she stopped, uncertain, but he walked ahead of her and opened the doors to a library. Hallie noticed the books and the massive, paper-covered desk. The room was a certain relief. This was familiar to her, the kind of room in which she might, at last, find her bearings.

And naturally this man would have a wonderful library. Of course he would.

She crossed to one of the shelves and stared blankly at the titles. At any other time she would have delighted in reading them, perhaps she *could* have read them, but just now she could not focus.

It was inconceivable that she could have mistaken one man for another. As she turned to face Marksley she realized how immediate recognition could be. She had thought that her first, negative impression of the Viscount Langsford, as R.E. Marksley, could only be wrong; she had determined to be fair, and the time she had granted to fairness had been her undoing.

Marksley seemed to find her countenance particularly absorbing.

"You were clearly surprised, Miss Ashton, when I entered the drawing room just now. Was this an appointment you honestly expected my charming cousin to keep?"

"I . . . had not thought about it."

His smile was slight. "I wonder whether you are very clever or exceedingly foolish."

Hallie skirted the shelves to move away from him. "Why must I be either, Mr. Marksley?"

" 'Tis very clever of you to ask." To her confusion, Hallie could feel a blush mount to her temples. "I would not have thought you his usual fare. But then, looks can be deceiving."

"You are speaking of your cousin. You imply that there must be more to me than meets the eye."

"On the contrary, Miss Ashton, my first impressions were entirely favorable. In that, apparently, I am deceived."

Hallie swallowed. He did not sound at all fond of his cousin. But his first impressions of her had been positive. That small encouragement lent her courage.

"I suppose you find it impossible to believe that he might have deceived me."

"In what way, Miss Ashton? Did he promise marriage?"

Hallie looked away, shaking her head. She could not tell him that his cousin had pretended to be R.E. Marksley, publisher of *The Tantalus*. This man probably believed she could not even read. Yet her silence fed Marksley's evident contempt.

"It seems your plans have not progressed as you might have wished." His smile was cynical. "You shall not nab a peer of the realm. But you may draw some Marksley blood for all that."

"I do not want you, sir."

"And I do not want you . . . lady. But how much more appropriate for you to say you will not *have* me." There was anger in his step as he moved away from her. "With thanks to you, everything I have worked to uphold is now held hostage. If not for that I would happily send you and your dyspeptic uncle packing." As he wheeled to her, Hallie instinctively clasped the shelves behind her. She would be compelled to marry someone, yet this forceful man was no more acceptable than his dissolute cousin.

"If your hands are tied now, sir, 'twas your cousin who saw to it, not I."

"I see. You were not, then, a willing participant in whatever indiscretion so incensed your uncle?"

"My uncle only heard of an indiscretion relayed to him by his cousin, Millicent Binkin, who, as you must have concluded, bears me some malice."

"Granted, the woman's eyesight—or her memory—is singularly poor. But did this malicious creature also invent the incident?"

"No. But she willfully misconstrued."

"Willfully misconstrued? You've an interesting way with words, Miss Ashton." Marksley surveyed her from head to toe. "I presume propriety is the sole reason for your family's eagerness?" When she defiantly raised her chin, he said, "Yes? But I understood you were alone with Reggie some time. And he is not usually slow." He moved closer. "Tell me, my dear, what on earth you were doing."

"We were conversing."

"Conversing? And the subject?"

"We discussed . . . land reform," she said softly and stared at the floor.

It was strangely pleasant to hear Marksley's laugh.

"Truly? How enterprising. You must indeed have exceptional skills in conversation, Miss Ashton, since that is a subject *I* could never convince my cousin to address. But you are clearly a young woman of many talents."

"Is this your purpose in cloistering me, sir? To insult me? I thought that you might wish to help, to find some way to avert an unacceptable outcome. We have little time to plan, to escape from this—" He interrupted her.

"I suppose it is one way of demonstrating your innocence in this matter. That you would even attempt to escape."

"I am innocent. And quite serious, sir." Again she tilted her chin. Marksley noted the movement; indeed, he examined her face minutely. Perhaps his perusal was another test of her character.

"Have you a proposal, Miss Ashton?" He was aware of the irony. Even had his lips not curved, the humor was there in his voice. But there was no time to spar with him.

"Nothing—now—other than delay."

"Delay. Ah, I see. So that you might have an opportunity to arrange your affairs with Reggie rather than myself." The humor had left his voice. He turned from her to his desk. "If he had troubled to inform any of us of his plans, we might reasonably judge how prolonged such a wait must be. I should imagine two weeks at a minimum, and possibly as long as two months. A daunting 'delay' in either case, if one is young. . .and in love."

He deigned to bow his head to her, ever so slightly, with a conviction that Hallie tried to ignore. It had occurred to her to try to explain herself, to deny that she felt any affection for his cousin, but Marksley, so clearly an insufferably superior being, was unlikely to listen.

When she stayed silent he at last said, "I will surprise you, Miss Ashton. I am willing to further your strategy and to assist you in delay, whether for two weeks or two months, as the case may be. Upon my cousin's return you may cry off and marry Reggie or choose someone else to your liking."

"They'll insist on an announcement."

"Then they shall have it. If the engagement is announced and the banns are published, that can consume several weeks at least. Since your uncle's aim is, pardon me, a certain legitimacy in the public eye, he should not object to our desire to forego the speedier license. And, as we have already faced the dilemma of two men named Marksley, your family might later claim an error in announcements that failed to distinguish between them. *Voila*! We shall at last be freed from this spectacle."

"You may be freed, sir, but I shall be forced to marry somewhere. And you seem to believe that an announcement is sufficient."

"Isn't it?"

"I fear there will be demands upon us, to meet certain expectations, for appearances' sake. My uncle is not easily appeased."

Marksley's satisfaction fled.

"That should not be necessary," he said stiffly. "Surely an announcement of an intention so permanent is enough of an appearance."

"I do not make these rules, sir."

"No. But you seem most eager to abide by them—once you have broken them."

Hallie turned from his glare to face a glass door and a small courtyard. "My uncle, Mr. Marksley, is certain that you are a scoundrel. *You*, sir. Not your cousin, but you. Should he remain convinced of both your guilt and your unwillingness to reform—to do right by me—he will have us trapped by a special license within hours."

"A special license is not so easily obtained."

"Believe me, sir," she said, turning to face him again, "my uncle would manage. He has been insisting on an early date."

Marksley considered her. "Your uncle has taken a fearsome position for one who cares for his niece."

"He believes himself to be acting responsibly."

"By disregarding your wishes?"

"He thinks he knows my wishes. In his view my actions, as described by Miss Binkin, have spoken for me."

"If you were to tell him—"

"You have heard me try," Hallie interrupted. It was too painful to revisit this ground. Her uncle was a good, solid man. He had done his best for her. In the years after the death of her father, that had not been easy. She could not blame him for doing what society expected of him. He had ever been a respectable, conventional man. That was the source of his strength—and his weakness. Her one desire had been that he might trust her instead of Millicent, but in his mind people, especially young people, must be expected to make mistakes. The best she might hope for now was that he would, in time, forgive her.

"You seem uncommonly intelligent, Miss Ashton," Marksley said. "It surprises me that you should see the rest of this matter so clearly—and yet have initiated it with such blindness."

"Blindness?"

"You have not told me what you think of my cousin. Presumably you found something to admire in him."

Rather something to admire in you, she thought, but she turned her attention once again to the garden.

"What I thought of him is of no consequence, Mr. Marksley."

"Ah, then I must imagine you were swayed by his looks and title. Love at first sight, as the poets would have it. He is a presentable young man. In fact, I believe he has earned a precious sobriquet. Brummell himself is said to have bestowed it. They call him the Gorgeous Langsford."

"To distinguish him from you, sir?"

He laughed shortly.

"You wound me, Miss Ashton. Indeed, I am not gorgeous, nor am I Langsford. My point, however, was that it is possible to see something quite lovely and yet be blind to its true nature."

Given his cousin's behavior, Hallie had no reason to disagree. But from the way Richard Marksley was looking at her, he might just as easily have been commenting on her own shortcomings.

"You are bitter, Mr. Marksley. Apparently you neither respect nor like your cousin. Do you covet the title? Or simply detest the man?"

"Neither, as it happens. 'Tis true Reggie has done little that anyone might find worthy of respect. I would have to include compromising young women among his more reprehensible acts." One dark eyebrow rose. "It is also true that I do not enjoy his company or seek his favor. We are very different." He shrugged. "My cousin . . . tries my patience. But I do not detest him. There are usually a few points to commend in even the most flawed of human beings."

"That is a relief, sir. I had suspected, from your manner, that there was no hope for me."

She thought he was tempted to smile, but she could not be certain, and his gaze moved away from hers.

"You would not be the first to have been mistaken in my cousin. There is, however, the not inconsiderable matter of how you acted upon first impression."

"I see I make no progress with you."

"On the contrary. Have we not progressed to the point of announcing our imminent marriage?"

Hallie found she very much resented his condescension.

"We are agreed, then?" she asked coldly.

"We are . . . resigned, Miss Ashton. We have been so ever since you entered this room alone with me. And for the next few weeks I shall endeavor to be available to court you. I hope you will pardon me, however, if I am not as openly demonstrative as your Reggie. I am capable of attempting to right some wrongs. I am not capable of dissembling to that extent."

Hallie's hands tightened against the muslin skirt of her gown. "You have an admirable sense of duty."

"Merely adequate, I assure you, for the quantity of demands presented. Yet for some reason, in speaking with you, I have been reminded of my mother. She would not have wanted any female, no matter how unworthy, to suffer at Reggie's hands. She suffered enough at his grandfather's."

The comment begged a question. But Hallie knew he had no intention of explaining, at least not to her, lowly creature that she was.

"Despite your . . . generosity in this instance," she managed, "few would have been as quick to term someone 'unworthy.' "

That watchful element returned to his gaze. "I must study your own character more closely then, Miss Ashton," he returned sharply, "so that I might improve myself. But come," he indicated the door, "we have been away long enough. At some point this drama must begin. It might as well be with your Miss Binkin."

"I do have one suggestion, sir, before we do so."

"And what would that be?" His expression was pleasant but shuttered. Hallie had the desire to shake him. She could tell she had been added to a list of obligations; she was but one more task to be crossed off in due course.

"It might appear odd that you never use my name."

"Yes, of course. And what is that name, Miss Ashton?"

She paused a second, tempted to tell him the whole. "Harriet. But everyone calls me Hallie."

"I am honored to be included amongst everyone . . . Hallie." He did not invite her to share the familiarity of his own name. The omission was deliberate. But perhaps he was right; she would not know him long enough to warrant its use.

"There is another matter, Miss . . . Hallie." As she turned to him, now close to him as she neared the door, Hallie looked directly up into his eyes. They were a deep, dark brown, intelligent and kind. Marksley was a reserved man, but not by nature cold. Were it not for this inauspicious beginning, Hallie sensed they might have been friends.

"I believe it important that we be the ones to control

this exercise. Not your uncle and certainly not my aunt. Henceforth, we may not always have the opportunity to discuss how best to proceed. I should hope to consult with you, but I have no doubt we will continue to be chaperoned. Add to that our own disinclination to spend much time together—" He paused. "I am asking for your trust, to make judgments when required, as there is no question that they will be. I am thinking of us both. If we are to manage the next few weeks without being hauled to the altar without warning, we must be perceived as acting in concert. We must be cautious."

She examined his face, which spoke so sincerely of a desire to deal responsibly with future difficulties. She did not doubt him. Richard Marksley would not presume upon the position and power society granted him. He had neither the interest nor the inclination to take advantage of her. He and his cousin could not have differed more.

"I appreciate your foresight, Mr. Marksley. And your consideration. Though I must tell you that with so much else decided for me, I question whether I have will enough remaining to object."

He surprised her by smiling, the first full smile she had seen on his face. Its effect on her was immediate . . . and disturbing.

"I very much doubt that is the case, Hallie. And to prove it I hope you will employ your will by choosing to call me Richard."

The concession pleased her, even if he were only practicing. As he again gestured toward the door, Hallie moved past him. But the heel of her shoe caught on the edge of a rug. Unbalanced, she reached to brace herself—and found Richard Marksley's strong right arm. She was aware that he drew her closer, steadying her. She could feel his arm tighten beneath the wool of his coat. And she could feel his warmth.

The door to the library swung open. Hallie, held in what could only have appeared to be an embrace, met the astonishment of the butler—and beyond him, the open-mouthed shock of her uncle and the Countess.

Hallie glanced up at Marksley, noting his clenched jaw.

"You see how easily 'tis done," she whispered, "with the simple opening of a door."

Chapter Three

Richard had reason to reflect on the comment the next morning. As he paced his library, Hallie Ashton's words accompanied his steps. "With the simple opening of a door," she had said, and truly it had been as simple as that: her uncle's instant eruption, Geneve's shock and puzzlement, Miss Binkin's owl-eyed stare. If he and Hallie Ashton had not been betrothed already, that near-embrace would have sealed their fate. "With the simple opening of a door!"

And yet nothing was simple, everything had changed—in his view, for the worse. The sunlight streaming in upon his desk looked very much as it had the previous morning, the day promised to be as fair as yesterday, he had enjoyed another fine ride across the park. Yet these were all surface similarities, for his mind was focused entirely on the matter at hand. He could not avoid the frustrating necessity to pay court to Miss Ashton over the coming weeks, unfortunately a critical time for *The Tantalus*.

Had she intended to confound him? Had she meant to imply that the circumstances tying her to Reggie were as "simple" or as innocent as what had transpired yesterday? What sort of a cousin was Miss Binkin then, to consign the girl to an unhappy future over such a trifling matter? Could he believe the woman could be so calculating? Could he believe Hallie Ashton?

He could see her face. With no effort at all he could see her face and her wide, gray eyes. She did not speak merely to justify herself, grasping at an excuse for her dalliance with Reggie. She had wanted him to understand. But he knew Reggie too well. However innocent and unusually wise Miss Hallie might be, she had succumbed as all the rest. It was the only reasonable explanation. Otherwise, a genteel young woman like herself would never have come within miles of the Gorgeous Langsford.

"Blast Reggie," he muttered, and flung wide the glass doors to the back garden. The morning was too cool for such ventilation. The curtains billowed wildly as Richard breathed in the bracing autumn air. But the brisk breeze and dancing drapes answered his need for release. At the moment he craved more than mere minutes in that liberated condition.

The knock at his library door was unwelcome, but Richard turned back to the room with a curt "Come."

As Gibbs opened the door, the elderly butler met his scowl with stiff dignity.

"Lord Jeremy has arrived," he announced, adding significantly, "with luggage."

"Ah—Gibbs." Richard rubbed his forehead and moved toward the door. "I just had his letter yesterday. In all the excitement I neglected to tell you. Lord Jeremy will be with us for a few days."

"Very good, sir. I shall have a room prepared at once."

"Thank you, Gibbs. Please send Jeremy in here. And see if Cook would prepare something? Tea, or . . . something."

"Certainly, sir." And Gibbs unbent sufficiently to make the briefest of bows before retreating. Within seconds Jeremy Asquith, fourth son of the Duke of Blythe, strolled into the room.

"I must say, Richard, Gibbs' welcomes seem to grow chillier and chillier. As do your rooms, by the way. Is this a new means of courting the muse? Or the latest in fashionable country living? 'Tis a devilish way to celebrate a birthday." He shivered as he stretched his hands before the blazing fire.

Richard closed the doors behind him, then smiled at his friend.

"Have a seat, Jeremy. Gibbs is miffed because I failed to tell him you were coming—a small oversight which I will explain. As for the temperature, I was attempting, unsuccessfully, to clear my head."

"Never say you are having problems with *The Tantalus*?"

"With Reggie." Richard drew his own chair to the hearth. "But first tell me what really brings you down to the country. A mere birthday, yesterday by the by, would never do so."

Jeremy smiled as he leaned back in his chair.

"I can always plead a desire for good company, Richard. The few people in town these days care little for horses, books, or a good laugh. I find I need at least one of the three to make life worthwhile."

Richard shook his head as he studied his friend. Jeremy Asquith was the very definition of lanky. Even while seated, his joints looked set to tumble apart, his arms and legs like so many pieces of an awkward puzzle—a deceptive appearance, because he had an appetite worthy of someone three times his girth and was accounted an accomplished shot and horseman. Jeremy's astonishing physique, combined with flaming red hair and a taste in clothing bordering on gaudy, always guaranteed him an initial, startled attention from those who had known him for years as well as strangers.

"I am in complete agreement, Jeremy. But as I find those to be the conditions in town all year 'round, you owe me another explanation."

Jeremy threw up his hands.

"I confess then, that I understood you have a uniquely lovely creature here in Surrey just now."

Richard tensed, wondering how Jeremy had heard about Harriet Ashton—then wondering when he himself had determined that she was lovely.

"The yellow nymph, my dear fellow," Jeremy supplied with a laugh. "*Neonympha lutea.* Their last little butterfly gasp before the winter." Jeremy's hobby, which he had pursued from his time at university with Richard, had earned him his greatest notoriety—he was one of the country's leading lepidopterists and a founding member of the London Naturalists.

Though he did not share his friend's passion, Richard understood its compulsions. But just now his problem weighed so heavily that the frown descended again.

"As it happens, your timing is faultless. This may well be my last gasp as well. You must congratulate me, Jeremy. I am to be married."

Jeremy's smile faltered.

"Not—Caroline?" he asked, his blue gaze sharpening.

Richard shook his head.

"No, thank God. Though you'll think me mad enough once I explain. You wouldn't have heard of the girl. Niece of a gaseous old gent over in Berkshire. A little ville called Tewsbury."

"Tewsbury," Jeremy repeated slowly. He looked concerned. "Richard, what have you done?"

"I have done nothing, Jeremy. I told you Reggie had been up to his old tricks, and this time he tossed me into a true bumblebroth." Richard thrust himself from his chair and paced again before the fire. "Apparently, he compromised the girl. Had she been just another of his indiscretions, we might have looked to her needs and tried to forget the matter. But this girl is a gentlewoman, with a terror of a cousin who caught them together and a bludgeoning uncle as guardian. Add Geneve's fears for her darling and the formula becomes quite knotty, with the predictable solution." His lips firmed bitterly. He was conscious of complaining, though Jeremy knew all.

"Who's the chit?" Jeremy asked.

"A Miss Harriet Ashton. An orphan, apparently. A vicar's daughter with only the tartar of an uncle to look out for her. If I didn't know she had been silly enough to fall for Reggie, I might even find it in my heart to pity her." When Richard finally met Jeremy's gaze he was surprised to see how intently his friend was studying him. And to his astonishment, it looked as though Jeremy attempted to hide some amusement. "Devil take it, you insufferable carrottop! What can you find laughable in this?"

Jeremy cleared his throat and looked away, idly brushing invisible lint from his spotless indigo coat. "Apologies, Richard," he said easily. "It's simply that I knew an Ashton. Tolliver—Tolly—Ashton. From Tewsbury, as it happens. I have mentioned him before. He joined the Light Horse after you were wounded at Vitoria and sent home. Took a ball at the Nivelle River and died two days later."

"And you find that humorous?" Richard demanded.

"No, no, just wondering whether this Miss Harriet might not be related. Seems likely they would be. Both from Tewsbury and all. I think I should like to meet her. As I recall, Tolly had a sister, or somesuch, who wrote some deucedly fine letters." His light gaze met Richard's again. This time he looked more curious than amused—as curious to watch Richard as to meet Miss Ashton.

"If you're to stop here with me for a while, you'll have opportunity enough. Miss Ashton and I will attempt to 'court' until Reggie returns from Ireland, where, of course, he's conveniently chosen to holiday."

"Another woman?"

"Horses," Richard corrected. "An abandonment you will no doubt commend in him."

"You forget, my friend, that I have yet to see your Miss Ashton."

Richard shrugged. "She has looks enough, I suppose. I was hardly in a frame of mind to do her justice. She speaks well, very well in fact. You will find her passable."

"Passable?" Jeremy smiled. "How droll. Is she truly such an antidote then, to leave Richard Marksley scrambling for words?"

In all truth Richard had only minutes before thought of her as lovely. Perhaps his confusion showed on his face, because Jeremy wisely refrained from pressing him.

"So—your engagement lasts only until Reggie's return?"

"Or failing that, for some three weeks from this Sunday, when the banns will be published. I must thank my good fortune that Ashton has not insisted on a special license."

"And if Reggie should decline to do his duty?"

"This he will not decline," Richard said bluntly. "I will delay for him. I will attempt, discreetly mind you, to find a substitute. I've asked Appleby to inquire. Perhaps I can convince some stripling that he desires a wife. But I shan't hang myself."

Jeremy cleared his throat.

"What of *The Tantalus?*" he asked, turning to survey the room as though its décor were of the utmost fascination.

"It will be difficult. But I don't foresee the necessity to spend every hour of the day with the girl. A man needs his own pursuits."

"Decidedly. Though you might find help from unexpected quarters. Particularly if Hallie—beg pardon, Miss Ashton—were to volunteer some of her time."

Richard stared at him in amazement.

"Miss Ashton volunteer her time! What are you on about? I suppose I might set a country miss to opening the post. But seriously, Jeremy, what can you be thinking?" His gaze narrowed. "And you called her Hallie. Do you know her, then?"

"What?" Jeremy blinked. "I thought that's what you called her. Or perhaps Tolly mentioned it. Just assumed this Ashton girl must be related. Hallie's a common enough name, ain't it?"

"Is it? I have never heard it before."

"You have scarcely been out amongst the smart set these past three years, Richard. It's all the crack for the young ladies to have their pet names. Miss Emmeline Potter is Mel, Lady Justine Smythe is Tina, the delectable Persis Kinnicott is Nicky—" He ticked them off on his fingers.

"I could wish you spent a bit less time in society, Jeremy. One Hallie Ashton is quite sufficient, thank you. If Geneve had not promised that this is the last thing she will ever ask of me, I would never have agreed to do as much."

"Wouldn't you, Richard?" Jeremy smiled. "Even to save the lady's honor?"

"What there is of it to save, you mean."

Jeremy looked stricken. "Oh, come, you cannot be serious. Never say that she and Reginald . . . that Reggie actually—"

"How can I know?" Richard asked. "Whatever she might say, whatever I might wish to believe, I know Reginald."

"Yes," Jeremy mused, and tapped the arm of his chair. "I should like to see Harriet Ashton, Richard. When do you plan to attend her?"

"Later today for tea, if you've a taste for it." Richard grinned. His friend was always eager for sustenance. "The Ashtons are guests at Penham. The Countess could not be moved to lend her son to this enterprise, but she deigned to volunteer a suite of rooms." His glance darkened as he turned once again to the glass doors. "I'll wager the little baggage is already cataloging the Hall's valuables."

"I cannot believe any relative of Tolly Ashton's would be so mercenary."

"Perhaps they are not related. And if anyone is constitutionally unable to think ill of a person it is you. I vow you would excuse even Caroline."

"There you are wrong, Richard," Jeremy said. A decided grimness settled over his features. "I sent Caroline to the devil many moons ago. Any charity I might once have granted her I withdrew when she married old Bellis. No true nonpareil could ever have cared for you and married him."

Richard turned back to him.

"Then perhaps I can rely on your good judgment with respect to Harriet Ashton. If I am being too harsh, Jeremy, if my instincts are unsound, you must tell me. And I trust to your cleverness, to help me devise an end to this predicament."

Hallie, seated in the sumptuous drawing room at Penham Hall, was distinctly unhappy. Her unease had nothing to do with the room, where pale yellow paper and tasteful gold and green appointments evoked bounteous fresh daffodils. Her discomfort had everything to do with the occupants.

"Did Reginald tell you anything of Surrey, Miss Ashton?" The Countess's voice, while still courteous, held a challenge.

"Nothing at all, milady."

"It is quite delightful, particularly at this season. I wonder that he did not speak of it."

"Why should you wonder at it, milady? As you have made clear, I have never met your son, Lord Langsford, only his cousin, Richard."

Lady Penham's lips firmed. Alfred Ashton glared a rebuke, but he could not touch Hallie now. She had agreed to do everything he wanted. After this, he could ask no more.

The butler announced the gentlemen. A second later, Hallie's gaze locked with Richard Marksley's. It puzzled her that she should again feel the same slight check to her composure. Here she sat, staring at Richard Marksley, when her first surprise should have been the presence of Jeremy Asquith.

"Lord Jeremy! What a treat for us!" The Countess eagerly extended both her hands. Hallie noticed that she was not above batting her eyes at a considerably younger man. "You're staying with Richard, of course. How delightful."

"Thank you, my lady. I stay only fleetingly. But the idyll will seem all the shorter when I leave your company."

Oh, do stubble it, Jeremy, Hallie thought. Again she caught Richard Marksley's glance and realized that he was thinking the same. The realization stunned her.

The countess was all aflutter. "Dear Jeremy. But of course you must return soon—for the wedding?" Her words froze everyone else in the room, though she was apparently oblivious to their effect. "Three weeks from Sunday, is that not right, Mr. Ashton?"

Hallie's uncle harrumphed and eyed Richard Marksley. "You remind me, countess, that Mr. Marksley and I have some business to discuss. What say you, Marksley?"

Hallie should have known her uncle would make even a polite tea unbearable. Her look entreated Jeremy.

"Perhaps I might walk out with Miss Ashton for a moment?" Jeremy offered. His smile was reassuring. "I believe we have some mutual acquaintance."

The countess sent her a swift, assessing glance. "Indeed? You astonish me, Miss Ashton. Truly. I shall ring for tea at once, my lord. Pray do not leave us long."

"Never, ma'am. Richard." Jeremy nodded to Marksley, who returned the gesture stiffly. Hallie rose to join Jeremy at the garden doors. "Miss Ashton, I believe we might find a tolerable stroll here just off the terrace," Jeremy said loudly enough for the others.

She let him lead her out onto the terrace. Even in the sun, the breeze remained chilly, but nothing short of an arctic blast would have sent her back into the house for her wrap. Millicent Binkin had already moved to watch them through the glass. Hallie defiantly turned her back to the windows and pressed her cold palms together.

"Jeremy," she said softly, "you must help me."

"Happily, m'dear," he said, too calmly for her taste. "I shall tell Richard the truth."

"Oh, no, Jeremy. Please. You cannot." She glanced back at the doors, where Millicent peered into the sunlight, her spectacles flashing ominously. "I must have that. I must have my life. If you tell him, 'twould ruin me."

"Hallie, I beg your pardon, but the thinking seems to be that that is already the case."

"Jeremy! How can you believe that? And of all people,

with that—that *egregious* Langsford?" She paused. "Is that what Richard Marksley believes? That I am ruined?"

"He doesn't know what to believe. You realize he is not in a position to act on his belief, regardless."

Hallie bit her lower lip and again turned from the house. She rubbed some warmth into her thinly-clad arms. Then the words spilled from her.

"I was fooled, Jeremy. I mistook Reginald for R.E. Marksley. Only I believe—in fact, I *know*—that he intended I do so. He was with a group of men at the coaching inn in Tewsbury. Reginald had just said something, and one of the others clapped him on the back and claimed the quip was 'worthy of R.E. Marksley' or 'just like R.E. Marksley'—something distinctly like that, in any event. They all laughed. The worst of it is that I sought him out. I was *glad* to meet him. At last! Even though I had promised myself not to try until the spring, until I can leave uncle." Hallie sighed and shook her head.

"I saw him while Millicent was speaking to the innkeeper's wife, nattering on about some church fete. When I went up to him he must have thought I was there at the inn, living there, some hostess or—oh, I haven't a clue what he thought. Before I even suspected his intention, he had pulled me through to a side room and kissed me, and there was Millicent. He may even have seen her coming." Hallie immediately checked to see if Millicent was still watching. "Then he deceived us, Jeremy. He claimed he was Marksley of *The Tantalus*. He intended we should all believe he was

Richard. That despicable man meant us to." Hallie could not prevent her shiver.

"Come, let's walk a bit." Jeremy took her arm. "Miss Binkin hasn't served you well in this, Hallie. But it's not beyond Reginald to have done this deliberately. You offered him the means, of course, but as you'll soon learn, he is spiteful to the core, and he hates Richard."

"Why should he?"

"No earthly reason. Just a simple matter of envy, if such can be simple. And fear—because Richard is actually the direct descendant at Penham."

"How is that possible?"

"Richard's father was the elder son, by several years. But he married, against his family's wishes, a charming Welsh lass—so I'm told—and was cut off. When he died, his brother, the present Earl—that would be Richard's uncle Cyril—managed to install Reggie as heir, with some balderdash about Reggie being six months older and the line not reverting. Had anyone been representing Richard's interests such stuff never would have held at law. The whole business probably sped the demise of Richard's mother, poor woman. Anyway, old Cyril and the Lady Geneve ended up responsible for Richard nonetheless. A constant reminder, no doubt, of their own ambitious maneuverings. They treated Richard accordingly. Yet Reggie was always jealous as a cat. Since you've met the two of them you know why." His grip on her arm tightened. "Hallie, you must tell Richard the truth."

"No." She shook her head. "There must be some other way."

"I don't believe so, m'dear. Richard will help you until Reggie's return. He believes he can prevail upon him. But I know, and you must suspect, that that irresponsible devil will never marry you. You cannot retreat to Berkshire, because your uncle believes you have been compromised. The news must be all over Tewsbury and more by now. You *must* marry—and who else might your uncle find acceptable? I would offer for you myself but fear you would not have me. Again."

"Jeremy—"

"I should not have mentioned it, I know. And you were right to refuse me. Though I could easily have felt myself blessed, you no doubt would have regretted it."

Hallie placed a hand upon his arm. "You hardly knew me. You offered because of Tolly, and for that I shall always consider you the best of friends. But you found a different path for me, and I have been more than grateful. Even happy." She looked away from him. "If only things were not such a muddle!"

"You must tell him. In the end it will have to be Richard, Hallie. Just as it has always been Richard—and always will be Richard." At her questioning glance he added, " 'Tis Richard Marksley who's kept the illustrious inhabitants of Penham afloat these many years. The Earl is infirm, near senseless much of the time, and Geneve has mind and heart only for her worthless son—the egregious Langsford, as you aptly term him. To be frank, Hallie, you are my friend. I will do what I can for you. But Richard is more. He is . . . a brother-at-arms."

"But I am desperate, milord."

"Why desperate? I should wish you happy. In my view, Richard is the catch. You should be praying for Reginald to continue west to America—and stay there until he's long in the tooth."

"I don't wish to marry at all. To marry someone I do not love. Who . . . cannot love me. Jeremy, you *know* me. How shall I continue?" She frowned and gazed out over the lawns.

Jeremy cleared his throat and turned her to face the way they had come. "You might continue quietly, as you have been, and continue to deceive him. No change there. Since I helped you in the first place I cannot very well object now. The only difference being, of course, that we shall be playing this game in close quarters. Or—" At Hallie's hopeful look he chucked her under the chin. "You can tell him. You would instantly be freed. I guarantee it. He would spirit you out of the country by camel if necessary; anything to place you out of harm's way. Do you not understand? 'Tis your attraction to Reginald he cannot fathom or forget. Your explanation will make that error clear." As they approached the door, Jeremy laughed softly to himself. "Forgive me, Hallie, but I cannot ignore the amusement in this."

"Is there any?" she asked tightly.

He nodded. "They may call Reggie the Gorgeous

Langsford, but 'tis Richard who fascinates the ladies. Why, I'd wager there are half a dozen misses in town who would eagerly forego their elevated prospects to join R.E. Marksley in more modest circumstances."

"Really?" Hallie asked, watching Jeremy's face. "He is . . . much admired?"

"Indubitably. The man has a honeyed tongue! They swoon when he speaks. He quotes poetry at 'em, don't you know." Hallie's gaze narrowed at Jeremy's smugly affected tone. "He would not attempt it with *you*, of course. I believe he has determined that you ain't his style. La! But imagine what a novelty that would be—to be wooed with one's own verse." As Hallie paled he reached to push her gently ahead of him through the door. He spoke softly to her ear. "Don't delay long, sweet. Richard Marksley has never been a slow top. He'll soon discover that the elusive Henry Beecham is very close indeed."

Richard could not have departed soon enough. He had watched Jeremy and Hallie Ashton return from the terrace. He was convinced that mere acquaintances could never have had so much to say to one another and in so animated a fashion. Throughout that subsequent torturous tea, though Miss Ashton had volunteered nothing at all, Richard felt justified in ascribing guilt to her every glance.

He did not speak to Jeremy for a good five minutes.

"You appear to know her rather well," he said at last, trying not to sound annoyed.

"Miss Ashton, d'you mean?"

"Of course I mean Miss Ashton!"

Jeremy smiled broadly and nudged his horse closer. "I see, Richard, that you neither understand nor approve my methods."

"Your methods? Your shameless pandering to Geneve and winkin' at Binkin?"

Jeremy laughed. "My dear fellow, what a sacrifice it was!"

"No doubt your prolonged tete-a-tete with Miss Ashton was a sacrifice as well."

"Never! Hallie Ashton is a pearl beyond price."

"A pearl? Ah, then you care a great deal for her, as you—"

"As I cared for her cousin. Richard, understand me. Do not confuse responsibility and friendship for something more. I did once, and was put promptly in my place. Besides," he added airily, "Hallie Ashton is beyond my touch."

"You're bamming me. You—a Duke's son! And she's a simple country miss. A vicar's daughter!"

Jeremy's glance was penetrating.

"You are remarkably obtuse in this, Richard. It must be the incident with Reginald that blinds you to the worth of the girl. Had she not been hidden away in tiny Tewsbury she'd have been a remarked beauty. Those lovely eyes! You must admit she has fine eyes, Richard, and an altogether striking face and form. 'Tis only her dress that is simple—a small matter of funds. She is intelligent, kind, amusing, spirited. In fact I think, and have thought for some time, that she is splendid."

Richard's horse shied. As he calmed the animal he looked directly at his friend.

"You're in love with the minx," he stated flatly. He did not like the possibility, and liked it even less that he had voiced it.

Jeremy sighed loudly. "You are not listening, Richard. Kindly trouble yourself to pay me some mind. And you have me thinking that you are overly eager to find fault with Hallie Ashton. You yourself must be smitten."

"Nonsense." Richard coaxed Apollo into a trot, compelling Jeremy to struggle to catch up. "You might remind yourself that your stated purpose in visiting is to locate your precious yellow nymph, not to play matchmaker. Reggie and Uncle Ashton have been effective enough in that sphere, thank you very much. If you truly wish to earn your room and board, *milord*, you will apply yourself to defeating their schemes." He turned to blaze at Jeremy, "Why on earth did you sit there and extol my few virtues to Ashton? You should have been persuading him that I'm the last man he should want for his niece!"

"I thought to reassure him, my dear chap, as you treated us to few words and a stony face for near an hour. Why, the old goat knew nothing of *The Tantalus*! I sought only to enlighten him. Can you blame me for choosing to sing your praises, with him glaring at you as though you were Lucifer's spawn?"

"Yes," Richard snapped. "I asked for your help. You understand the situation. Anyone would think you want me to marry—" Instantly, he fixed Jeremy with an accusing stare. "That's it, isn't it, you sneak of a turncoat. The wench is enceinte and you have decided to make me a papa."

Jeremy, magnificent in his violet satin waistcoat and billowing fountain of a cravat, drew himself up in the saddle. His nose reached an exaggerated height. "That is beneath you, Richard. Hallie Ashton is a lady, incapable of that . . . of such conduct. She is as blameless in this as you are. I demand an apology—or satisfaction."

Richard surveyed him, in all his glorious indignation, and had to smile. "Easy, my friend. As you might imagine, I have had quite enough of Ashtons and Marksleys. The possibility of one more could not be overlooked."

"In Hallie's case it must be."

"Then I stand corrected, Jeremy. As I now know you for her champion," he added, "I shall refrain from such charges. No doubt Miss Ashton does indeed share Reggie's interest in—what was it? Land reform. Yes, land reform."

"Cut line, Richard," Jeremy said. "You make it irritatingly clear that you do not want Miss Ashton. But you should remind yourself of the corollary. Miss Ashton does not want you."

"She wants a lord."

"She wants no one."

Richard fell silent. If that were true, he should not

feel so incomprehensibly vexed. Jeremy was being less than candid, a difference in him that could only be traced to Hallie Ashton. The woman had to be hiding something; females did not huddle with the Viscount Langsford to discuss agriculture.

"Jeremy, you are always welcome at Archers. But perhaps we should not mention Miss Ashton again."

"As you wish." There was a marked chill in Jeremy's voice. "Would you prefer that I move on?"

"No, I do not *prefer*. I merely choose to avoid the subject of Miss Ashton."

"That might be a bit of a challenge. Had you forgotten that we are joining the ladies for a drive Saturday?"

With a frustrated glance at Jeremy, Richard swore softly and spurred Apollo ahead.

Chapter Four

Hallie had been ready for some time. After dismissing the Countess's abigail, who had fussed over a reluctant charge's limited wardrobe and equally limited patience, she had sought one of the private sitting rooms at the front of Penham Hall. There she attempted to write in her journal, a habit that had been neglected shamefully over the past week. Yet even with quiet and the best of intentions, she found she could not concentrate.

The hard little knot of an idea, the very beginnings of a poem, resisted the plucking necessary to untangle it. As a result the pages held half-starts and broken fragments of phrases, hinting at the whole, but not yet forming a smooth fabric of thought and feeling.

She knew why she could not work. For the twentieth

time within as many minutes, her gaze escaped to the drive, where she anticipated Richard Marksley. The man thought her little better than a lightskirt; even if she were the most proper young woman in England, he would still question everything about her. Yet she sat here watching for him. To be judged so harshly, and by Richard Marksley of all people, was galling.

Abruptly she rose and turned away from the window. At least she would have the satisfaction of delivering her message to Jeremy. Her uncle and Millicent might keep her a virtual prisoner, but she had thought of a way out of this trap. She had every intention of leaving the country.

She had enough money for passage to Ireland, or even perhaps to America, if she were to tap Henry Beecham's tidy sum. Marksley had stressed to Beecham in more than one letter that the poet could claim his earnings at any bank with a signature and his letters of credit. Hallie had not needed the money; she could not have invested it and her uncle would have noticed unusual spending in any event. She had feared as well that by claiming the funds she would reveal her identity to Marksley. She had even thought of the payments as bait.

Now she would snap at that lure. But she had devised a means to have someone else—a man—obtain her proceeds for her. She had determined to ask George.

George Partridge had last stopped to see her three months before in Berkshire. A renowned linguist and mutual friend of hers and Jeremy's, George had traveled widely, researching the world's unique tongues. She believed he was now transcribing the Romany speech of the country's gypsies, though she had no inkling as to his location. She must trust Jeremy to find their friend and deliver her message. George, she knew, would have no difficulty in copying her signature as "Henry Beecham." George could imitate any accent and any hand.

Hallie convinced herself that George would be happy to do this small favor. She had, after all, persuaded him to send one of his articles on language to Marksley and *The Tantalus*. He had found an admiring audience, as she had known he would.

She looked again at the drive. It was troubling to discover how easily she had learned to identify Richard Marksley even from a distance. Something in the set of his shoulders distinguished him from Jeremy and all others.

She took her time collecting her things and returning them to her room. Once she had donned her pelisse and gathered a bonnet she knew she was more than acceptably late, but the recognition did not prompt her to hurry. She had so few days left, so little time; she could not bear to rush the minutes. She did not question that she thought in terms of time left with Marksley.

Millicent Binkin met her in the foyer. Hallie had scarcely addressed a word to the woman since the disastrous intrusion at the Tewsbury inn. Yet Millicent did not seem to resent Hallie's uncivil silence, nor to feel any regret for committing her young cousin in such a questionable manner.

"You have certainly dawdled, missy. Although, given the sorry state of your wardrobe, one would hardly credit it. You must remind me to help you select several new day gowns. You look a proper dowd."

"The gentlemen will hardly wish for my company, then," Hallie said. "I shall leave you to them." She started to turn away, but Millicent grasped her arm.

"My dear," she said repressively, "These theatrics are childish. You must remember that all of one's actions have consequences. Neither I nor the gentlemen outside desired this situation."

"And that you know to be a lie, Millicent," Hallie retorted, chafing at the too-tight grip on her arm. "Why are you permitting this sham to continue? Why compel Richard Marksley to stand for his cousin?"

"You were irretrievably compromised—"

"Only in *your* eyes, dear cousin. You were both source and sound. You know you have much to answer for in all this. When Reginald Marksley returns you shall appear quite ridiculous."

"You are not usually dimwitted, Harriet. Had I believed for one moment that the Viscount would claim you, I would never have settled for Mr. Richard."

"*You* would not! Millicent, you take too much upon yourself. This is none of your affair."

"But it is, my dear." And her cousin's glance was sharp. "I have ensured an acceptable match for you. An eminently acceptable match. You were in a fair way to being overlooked. No season, no prospects. Only your endless scribblings. Now you will be established, and very well at that."

It was unseemly, to be arguing here in the foyer, with their escorts mere feet beyond the door. Yet to have Millicent Binkin so openly confess her scheming, without regret or shame, was more than Hallie could abide.

"We will discuss this later, Millicent," she managed, twisting free of her cousin's clutch. "It is outrageous that you would let all of us live this lie. I shall most certainly tell uncle."

"But he already knows, dear," Millicent said.

Hallie clenched her fists. She had not known she was such a drain on her uncle's household as to be foisted like chattel upon a stranger. She did know she was shaking, but she could not seem to stop.

The front door opened abruptly to Richard Marksley. Hallie could feel some force in him of anger or impatience. That consciousness made her tremble all the more.

"Ladies." Though his dark gaze revealed little, Hallie had the distinct impression that he had overheard them. "Are you ready to set out?"

"Thank you, Mr. Marksley. We are indeed." Millicent stalked on through the door, her short, stout figure squeezed into an unflattering patterned muslin. Hallie glanced up at Richard Marksley's face, to find him coldly eyeing Millicent Binkin's retreating back.

"I believe you are unlucky in your relations," he said, for her ears alone, and Hallie again suspected he had heard that conversation. Though he continued to look grim, he offered her his arm. "Shall we attempt once more to make the best of things?"

"I . . . prefer to stay in this afternoon."

One dark eyebrow arched.

"Never tell me you are a coward, m'dear. Are you as averse to high-steppers and speed as I suspect your cousin to be?"

Hallie, still shaky, let her hand seek his sleeve. She was grateful for his support. And she was grateful for something more. It pleased her to think he could share her dislike for Millicent Binkin. They were partners in that, if in nothing else.

In the drive, Jeremy was just helping Millicent into the back of the barouche, an exercise in agility that displayed neither to graceful advantage. As only Jeremy's horse stood saddled nearby, Hallie surmised that Richard Marksley intended to drive.

"I thought you might choose to ride up with me," he said. "The Earl's team is spirited but responsive. If you are so inclined, you might like a turn at the ribbons."

Hallie readily agreed to sit forward with him, something she would have preferred over Millicent's company in any event. As Marksley took her hand to help her up, Hallie felt the warmth of his own, even through their gloves. She bit her lower lip as she concentrated on her footing.

"Miss Ashton is a remarkable hand," Millicent supplied unbidden. "And she has been riding from the time she could walk. She is esteemed quite a horsewoman."

"Indeed?" Marksley murmured. Millicent's isolation in back had been intended. At the moment, Hallie wished her cousin further—somewhere near the ends of the earth.

As Marksley took his seat beside her, Hallie realized she was holding her breath. She willed herself to breathe easily, and glanced over at Jeremy.

"You prefer the saddle, Lord Jeremy?"

"If I am not invited to drive, Miss Harriet. I suspect Richard would be less indulgent were I his passenger."

"Only too correct, Jeremy. You would have Penham's cattle in the ditch before permitting another vehicle by you."

"Oh come, Richard. I am not that demonic. And the traffic out here in the country is nothing to speak of."

"Truly, Jeremy? And what would you call that lumbering contraption ahead of us?"

Jeremy made play of peering at a monstrous hay cart in the lane beyond the gates.

"Demme, if it ain't a thatched cottage. Well, Richard, if you aim to amble along behind *that* all afternoon, you may drive with my blessing." Jeremy dropped back to engage Millicent politely in some tedious twaddle about the countryside.

The carriage easily passed the hay cart and moved beyond neatly scythed fields and the occasional pasture of sheep. The sun was bright, the afternoon unexpectedly balmy.

Hallie, conscious that she had much to say but little inclination to speak, concentrated on watching the horses and Marksley's capable hands on the reins. At times her attention strayed to his profile. He had well-cast features, a firm jaw, a fine nose. Though she decided he could not claim to be as gorgeous as his celebrated cousin, he had a manly refinement that was attractive. Combined with the confidence that seemed characteristic, he was a compelling gentleman. He had to be for her to find his face so intriguing.

"Is everything in its proper place?" he asked suddenly.

"I . . . certainly. Pardon me." She shivered and glanced away.

"Are you cold, Miss Ashton?"

"No," she said, again turning to him. Her own gaze challenged his reversion to 'Miss Ashton.' To her irritation, he seemed all too aware of her reaction. Those eloquent lips were amused.

"The air tends to be chill in this hollow, Miss Ashton. On many a warm summer's day we have fog in here at noon."

"You frequent the spot then, Mr. Marksley?"

"Excessively." But now he was smiling. Hallie had thought him an attractive man before; now the smile persuaded more than her thinking.

She grasped the rail on her left and settled her reticule on her lap. She reminded herself of her strategy—to talk to Richard Marksley about his *Tantalus*. If she were destined to betray herself, she would do so because of what she knew and might unthinkingly reveal. She was a reader; she knew his journal. How natural, then, to speak with Richard Marksley about his library and his work. She would, she thought, confuse him—to the extent that she reasonably might be assumed to know most of what Henry Beecham knew.

"You are the editor of *The Tantalus,*" she ventured. The opening gambit made her feel small. "I should like to know more about your work."

"In the sense of how I occupy my time?"

"Yes. I . . . have seen most recent numbers. You write a letter introducing each."

"That letter is all that I do write, as I have little talent for the craft. I have prided myself, however, on selecting work of interest to readers."

Jeremy, posting alongside, brought his horse closer. "It is a talent in itself to recognize and foster it in others, do you not think so, Miss Harriet? Indeed, Richard is supremely talented—when I think of all he has brought to the rest of us." He winked at her, which made her blush.

Marksley frowned. "Thank you, Jeremy," he said, but his swift look at his friend was guarded. At the look, Jeremy dropped back again to Millicent's side.

Hallie was grateful for Jeremy's removal. He was an annoying reminder of her duplicity.

"And do you approach your authors with requests for stories and criticism?"

"They are not my authors, Miss Ashton, although there are those few upon whom I can rely. Yet to answer your question—it would be foolish for me to await material in the post. The serendipity involved in doing so would make a regular bimonthly printing quite impossible. Subscriptions are our largest source of funds, after all."

"And the other sources?"

He glanced quickly at her. She had forgotten that ladies did not discuss finances with gentlemen. As Henry Beecham she had never had a qualm.

"I myself am one source, Miss Ashton. Along with the occasional gift. I am afraid *The Tantalus* must qualify as a gentleman's hobby, as it rarely returns any monetary profit."

And now I shall use your precious money, Hallie thought, *to flee you.* But he must have construed her silence as criticism.

"My hands may be stained by ink, Miss Ashton," Marksley added, "but, as I never trouble to pay myself, I avoid the stigma of engaging in trade. Such distinctions affect the standing of an Earl's nephew, no matter how material his more gentlemanly duties."

There was a tight line to his lips. Hallie would have pursued the nature of his other duties, and learned just how he felt about his aunt and uncle, but that bitter expression intimidated. Ironically, *The Tantalus* presented the safer subject.

"My uncle is not a subscriber to your journal," she said, "but I read it at the circulating library in Tewsbury. It is extraordinarily popular. I have always enjoyed the mixture of articles and stories."

"Thank you, Miss Harriet. And do you have a favorite? Do you prefer a story or commentary?"

"I . . . have no favorites," she said, working her shaking fingers into the folds of her skirt. "Although I appreciate the selection of poetry."

"Ah, yes. We have published some excellent poetry." Now at last on a clear, flat stretch of road Marksley loosened the reins, encouraging the team to a brisker pace. Hallie's glance at Jeremy noted his relief at the change. He had surrendered in patience to Millicent's inconsequential remarks. Now he coaxed his mount to keep pace with the carriage.

Richard Marksley, with the team well in hand, glanced her way again. "Does a particular style of poetry appeal to you, Miss Harriet?"

"All poetry," she said and chanced a smile. But Marksley was no longer looking at her. His brow was furrowed.

"Perhaps you have seen some of Henry Beecham's poems."

"I am . . . not certain."

"Quite." It was a very chilly little word. Apparently engrossed in managing the team, Marksley lapsed into an extended silence.

Hallie thought Jeremy had heard that last exchange; she thought she heard his impatient snort. Or perhaps that was from his now straining steed.

She pointedly kept her gaze on the road ahead.

She knew why she had declined to discuss Henry Beecham; she was wary of divulging too great a familiarity with the poet. Yet she had managed instead to sound witless. Surely her greatest protection from discovery was her sex, whether or not she claimed any knowledge of Henry Beecham. And she did not like Marksley's silence. She did not like it at all.

"I do recall reading something recent by Henry Beecham," she said. "About the ocean—'a wash of blue, sweet surge of sea, earth's answer to eternity. . . .' Well, I forget the rest. But it was very nice." This time she was certain it was Jeremy who snickered, not his horse.

"Better than Byron, eh, Richard?" Jeremy suggested wickedly.

Marksley, concentrating on the horses, was frowning. But Hallie sensed he was thinking of Beecham, not the team. She wondered whether Marksley published the poems merely to gratify an insatiable, indiscriminate public. Perhaps he needed only to fill his pages.

"Did you not like it?" she asked, at once uncertain.

"Yes, I liked it. I liked it very much indeed, confound the man."

Jeremy laughed.

"What is it, Jeremy?" Marksley snapped. "Have we chanced upon some of your butterflies?"

"Unfortunately not, my friend, although a trap of sorts has most certainly been set."

Marksley favored Jeremy with a scowl, than looked over his shoulder at Millicent. Hallie's cousin had managed to fall asleep, her chins nestled comfortably into her shawl.

"Would you care for a turn at the ribbons, Miss Harriet?" he asked. "This stretch of road affords a fine, smooth run."

She nodded and took the reins from him, feeling at once all thumbs as his warm, gloved hands temporarily cradled her own. There may not have been butterflies about the road, she decided, but some had apparently settled along her midriff.

"Loose them, Hallie," Jeremy urged, and she needed no second prompting. The grays had responsive mouths and glorious, balanced strides. They flew ahead, fulfilling her own need for freedom, flashing along unchecked and powerful. She was conscious then only of the bright, encompassing afternoon light—a light that reflected from the fields and the open road and the very earth itself. The pounding of the horses' hooves delighted her. She wanted to take in and swallow the speeding air.

Her bonnet slid behind her, the wind bringing a sharp sting to her cheeks.

They must have run two miles before Hallie at last pulled them up. Flushed with the flight, she restored the reins to Marksley, then attempted to resettle her bonnet atop her windblown hair.

"Well done, Miss Hallie," Marksley said. She considered it a victory of sorts that he condescended to call her Hallie once again. He was examining her face with curiosity. "They were bred for speed and are not easily slowed. Who taught you to drive?"

"My cousin Tolly. He was very good."

"Tolliver Ashton was a splendid hand, Richard," Jeremy said. He was out of breath as he reached them. "You'd have liked him."

"Undoubtedly." But Richard Marksley was studying Hallie's high color with an intensity she found disconcerting. She told herself it was absurd—absurd to believe the name 'Henry Beecham' might be branded upon her forehead.

"You will . . . kill us . . . all . . . Harriet," Millicent gasped from the back. "She should not . . . be allowed . . . to sport with . . . your team, sir."

"Why ever not, Miss Binkin? You yourself claimed she is a remarkable hand. Your cousin is as skilled as any man I know."

"She is not a man, Mr. Marksley."

Hallie wanted to laugh aloud. To Richard Marksley she *was* a man, in the person of Henry Beecham. But that unhappy grimness had settled again upon Marksley's face. He directed the horses down a winding section of road.

"She is not a man, Miss Binkin. And all of us are here precisely because she is not. Should you truly wish her to refrain from driving you must raise the matter with her uncle. Until he indicates otherwise, his niece—my *betrothed*—is welcome to handle this team. She has demonstrated her competence."

Hallie blessed him silently. Her eyes must have mirrored something of her pleasure in rebellion because Richard Marksley lent her a smile.

They discussed books. While Millicent settled, sulking, in back and Jeremy amused himself with enthusiastically pronouncing on every humble roadside weed, they discussed what Hallie had most recently read and intended to read. In such conversation she found little reason for subterfuge; there seemed small likelihood that one's reading might reveal clues of too singular a nature. If Marksley sometimes met her gaze with a puzzled one of his own, Hallie attributed it to the usual amazement that a woman might appreciate more than the fashion plates.

When they at last returned to Penham, Hallie believed she had acquitted herself well. He could not have found her all that tedious. And heady with the thought that her secret was now safe—that she could mention *The Tantalus* or even poetry without inviting detection—she smiled as Richard Marksley helped her down from the high seat. She dared hope that the time spent awaiting the Viscount's return might at least be companionable. She did not wish to be at war with Richard Marksley.

Watching Jeremy haul Miss Binkin from the barouche, Hallie belatedly remembered her note for George Partridge. As Marksley moved to speak to the groom, who was steadying the horses up front, she drew the letter swiftly from her reticule. When Millicent looked down to straighten her skirts, Hallie handed the note to Jeremy.

In her scratch across the vellum he clearly recognized the addressee; he glanced at her expectantly. But Richard Marksley had already turned back towards them. He had most certainly noticed Jeremy's questioning glance at her. And Jeremy was slow to pocket the letter.

Marksley's look stung. Hallie knew that she was once again suspect. But to her surprise, Jeremy drew the open rebuke.

"I see I have been *de trop* this afternoon, my lord," Marksley said. The words were light, but his expression was not. "Perhaps you have not been entirely honest regarding your reason for visiting Archers. If either you or Miss Ashton chooses to release my family from this arrangement, I should be much obliged."

With a dark glare at Hallie he bowed stiffly and strode for the stables.

"A very rude young man," Millicent commented with a sniff, and started up the steps toward the door. Hallie looked pleadingly at Jeremy.

"You must find George," she urged softly. "I need his help."

"For what, m'dear? A translation of Urdu?"

She frowned.

"This is not a joking matter, Jeremy. He must sign for me as Henry Beecham at the bank."

"Sign for you? Hallie, you must permit me—"

She shook her head. "You are known everywhere. The Duke of Blythe's family! 'Twould be like asking the Regent himself to pose as Beecham."

"Then at least take the funds?"

"No, Jeremy. You know I cannot. Someone would hear of it, and I would trade one form of notoriety for another. 'Tis best to find George. I have explained all in the letter. I believe he was heading west with his gypsies."

"Then I go west as well, m'dear. Especially now that Richard threatens to bar the doors to me. Though I do hate to leave this promising situation."

"Promising?" Hallie's voice rose. "What can you mean?"

"Why—I do believe the Honorable Richard is jealous." At his slow, suggestive smile, Hallie's face warmed.

"Harriet," Millicent commanded from the door and Hallie gratefully fled.

Chapter Five

Richard slowly sipped his tea and stared out at the rain. The fine weather had ended last night. The drive had puddled and the road would most probably be worse. As he anticipated the visit to church that morning, he thought a difficult trip would prove fitting. It would be his first attendance at a service in months, and all for publishing the banns.

Jeremy had departed early, before Richard even came in to breakfast, which was, as usual, very early indeed. He had been surprised that Jeremy, with his habitual good humor, had not found some way to tease him about yesterday's incident, to ignore his display of temper. It had been unwise to reproach the two of them, despite appearances. He realized that he had come to rely unthinkingly on Jeremy's capacity to bear abuse.

Certainly if confronted by similar pique in another, *he* would have found pressing reason to leave. Yet Jeremy had never taken him seriously before, much to his own unending irritation. Why should he do so now—and before breakfast?

"The devil take them," Richard muttered, staring moodily at the walls of his dining room. He had not taken stock of his surroundings for a while, and now wondered if, though a bachelor, he would be expected to entertain his betrothed and her family here at Archers. But the prospect was unwelcome—his aunt must be convinced to find more suitably staged settings for the next few acts. Apart from having his housekeeper pay additional attention to the draperies, he would not alter a thing. If Harriet Ashton desired to make a splash, she would simply have to wait for Reggie.

Not that she seemed to crave such fripperies, but one could never know about women. Their considerable requirements had confounded him before. Years ago he had believed Caroline Chalmers shared his interests. She had been intrigued by his indifference to most of the *ton's* pursuits, including, at the outset, Caroline Chalmers herself. She had claimed relief in his preference for distance and rational conversation. In Caroline he had been thoroughly mistaken. Surely Harriet Ashton had her own indecipherable whims.

Yet there was something about the girl, something in that clear gaze that hinted at humor and reflection. She was well-read, she refrained from senseless comment, her voice was low and pleasant. She had quoted Pope. She was unquestionably intelligent. He conceded it crossly, placing the cup and saucer on the table with a clatter.

Despite such signs of sanity, she had still tossed her cap at Reggie.

The carriage was ready and waiting. Richard cloaked himself to Gibbs's satisfaction and took the two umbrellas proffered, he assumed, as insurance should Miss Ashton and Miss Binkin beg a ride home. He knew his intended would do no such thing, but Miss Binkin very well might. After the banns were announced, even after that annoyingly public declaration, they would be expected to show some continuing preference for each other's company.

The village church, a tidy stone building of disputed history and considerable weathered charm, stood back from the road. As Richard made his way up the flagstone walk, beneath the looming, age-old oaks, the drizzle renewed. Unfortunately, the rain in no way dampened the curiosity of the many neighbors, tenants, and tradesmen he had known for nearly two decades. In foisting this deception on them, Richard felt he was committing a crime.

The church was full. Richard noted the fact, conscious that perhaps the Earl of Penham should propose building an addition. He settled along the aisle toward the back. Then his gaze found Harriet Ashton.

He had been irritated with her, even angry, yet anger

was not what he felt when he met her anxious gaze. As he took his seat he pondered his reaction, attempting to identify the unusual sensation. When the answer finally occurred to him it was a surprise.

He wished to protect Hallie Ashton.

With the thought, he managed to look everywhere other than at her. It was taking family responsibilities a bit too far, in addition to everything else, to now feel protective. Over the centuries countless others had wed to pay a debt, to preserve an ancient, respected name, to extend property or produce an heir. That line must be strong in him that he would contemplate surrendering so much else to fulfill it. Certainly the Earl of Penham had done nothing to deserve such a sacrifice. And Reggie would never trouble to reflect on any of it; the heir apparent would sneer at the outmoded notion of honor. Reggie thought the virtues were for others, but the vices . . . *those* had always been well worth pursuit.

What should he make of this baffling desire to shield the winsome Miss Ashton? Richard kept his gaze averted from her simple straw bonnet. He had almost convinced himself that she was an innocent victim of Reggie's transgressions. After all, Reggie had used others before. Miss Ashton could not have anticipated danger.

As the vicar's voice droned on, Richard looked ahead to where his aunt sat in the Penham box. It was in front, and she sat there alone, looking as misplaced as a flamboyant tropical bird, one that had inexplicably settled among sparrows. She had exhibited no restraint in her choice of dress. Her bright yellow turban must have blocked the view of those even three rows behind her. The mystery lay in why she had troubled to come.

Richard stifled a sigh. It was unfortunate, this public affirmation of a lie. But a special license would have been worse; he and Miss Ashton would not have retained the luxury of time.

As he caught the too-curious gaze of one of Denhurst's busybodies, Richard quickly looked away. He stared at the small church's single stained glass window, depicting John the Baptist in the wilderness. Richard's inspection focused sympathetically on the innocent lamb at John's feet.

When the vicar obligingly read the banns, Richard's attention returned immediately and painfully to the proceedings. The low murmur of the congregation surrounded him, trapping him. Had the service not then been nearing its close he would have excused himself, for lack of air.

He glanced at Hallie Ashton. Her features were pale but composed. If she could look so, he knew he could not shame her.

"My dear boy," Squire Lawes was upon him at once, pounding him on the back even as he attempted to rise from the pew. "This is wonderful news. You must bring Miss Ashton and her family to supper. A celebration, what? Perhaps Tuesday?"

"Tuesday? I regret to say, sir—"

"Tuesday would be lovely, Squire," Geneve accepted

quickly. Her gaze cautioned Richard. "I know Miss Ashton and her uncle would be delighted. We shall all come together. Your lady is always such an incomparable hostess."

The Squire beamed. "You are too kind, Lady Penham. Our honor, to be sure. Shall we say six? Augusta does prefer country hours."

Richard bowed and thanked him, then offered an arm to his aunt.

"Surely it will not be necessary to accept every invitation, madam," he protested in low tones. "Or do you feel some need to gratify the curiosity of the populace?"

"You must begin sometime, Richard. You will, after all, be marrying the girl."

"Ah! We differ there. I believe my commitment extends only to *pretending* to be marrying the girl."

Geneve managed to smile and nod to an acquaintance, but Richard could see that the smile was forced.

"Three weeks from today, Richard, you shall have to abandon all thoughts of pretense."

"On the contrary. Three weeks from today, once my messengers have succeeded in locating him and dragging him home by the ears, your son will have to abandon all pretense. And some mammoth measure of his freedom."

Geneve bristled. "You are serious?"

"Indeed."

"I cannot believe this of you. That you could be so ungrateful! And I had your promise—"

"Marksley," Alfred Ashton had managed to work his way to their side as they exited the church. "We may not have begun well, but I wish to shake your hand now in the hopes of a better future."

As Geneve's blue eyes still blazed indignantly, Richard shook Ashton's hand. Hallie's uncle would be even happier when he snared a viscount.

"And Miss Harriet?" Richard asked, aware that his betrothed had not followed them out into the damp.

"Receiving some well-wishers. Ah! But here she is. Well, let us see the two of you together."

Richard thought her gray spencer appropriate for the occasion. Against the gray stone walls of the church, under the gray sky, with her own gray eyes watching him in that disconcerting way, he thought he would have chosen to have her painted just so. Whatever brightened her cheeks and hair and lit her eyes from within seemed that much fresher in this dreary setting.

He moved to stand closer to her and was instantly conscious of a sensation of touching, though they stood some distance apart. He cleared his throat.

"What did you think of the service?" he asked.

"I confess I paid scant attention to the service."

"And what could have distracted you, I wonder?"

As her gaze shot intently to his, he knew she had been thinking about *him.* With that recognition, they stood silently for some seconds in unintentional communion.

"Where is Lord Jeremy?" she asked at last.

He could not have explained his reaction. But the question reminded him of his earlier apprehensions, and the suspicions that roused feelings unhappily akin to jealousy. With some low and inarticulate demure, he excused Jeremy's absence, then lapsed again into silence—this time decidedly less easy.

"I wish—" Hallie Ashton began as the others chattered around them. "Well, it is just that there is something so very final about a churchyard. There is no escaping." She indicated the small graveyard. "Thomas Gray understood: 'Each in his narrow cell for ever laid.' "

He turned to her, unwillingly drawn by the power she seemingly had to charm him without effort. But now the vicar was upon them, and Richard rallied.

"I am afraid," he said, glancing pointedly at the Countess, "that 'til death do us part' is included in the script."

"You have always had a fondness for the quips, Mr. Marksley, have you not?" the vicar observed dryly. "Perhaps if we were to see you here more often—"

"Which reminds me, Mr. Mayhew," Richard said quickly, "that I have indications the Earl is considering your needs for a larger church. Perhaps you might come see me sometime soon about a likely remedy."

The vicar, managing to look stunned and joyous at once, mumbled thanks as Geneve pulled Richard to the side.

"Cyril has never mentioned such beneficence," she hissed.

"You are correct, ma'am. To date he has not. But I have every confidence he shall. 'Tis needed and appropriate. I should have noticed before."

" 'This is . . . extortion, Richard." Geneve actually stamped her foot.

"No, madam. This is generosity. But you should not be surprised that I am capable of schemes of my own." Pleased with managing even such a small victory, he left her abruptly and turned back to the Ashtons. Vicar Mayhew and his wife and nephew had been added to Squire Lawes's supper party; Richard feared that the night's gathering would grow larger. Yet as he watched Hallie Ashton in conversation, he admitted to a great curiosity. She was not a quiet country mouse. She was polite, yes, but the quick wits he had noted in her were not accidental. He wondered if the various diversions of company might topple her guard, and lead her to reveal more of herself.

In the end, the night's party was not large. As they took their seats for the meal, Augusta Lawes and her husband hosting the two ends of the table, Richard Marksley sat at Augusta's right, Hallie on the Squire's right. They were as far away from each other as they could possibly be. Between them were Hallie's uncle, young Phoebe Lawes, Vicar Mayhew and his wife, Eleanor, the ever-present Miss Binkin, and the Mayhews' nephew, Archibald Cavendish.

The Countess of Penham did not attend. Having forced the invitation upon them, she had discovered, typically, that her ailing husband's needs obliged her to send sincerest regrets.

"Now, Miss Ashton, you must tell us all about yourself." Augusta Lawes beamed down the length of the table. "Have you had a season?"

Hallie was very aware of the interest the other guests exhibited in the answer. Phoebe Lawes in particular looked as though she enjoyed the question, being—as she was—certain of Hallie's response.

"No, ma'am. I've not had that pleasure. I have only visited London for short periods, and not during the season."

"But you have had an opportunity to shop and to attend the theater and such. Phoebe is so looking forward to spending next spring there with my sister."

Phoebe, looking immensely pleased with herself, shot a superior glance at Hallie. "London must be deadly dull when no one is there," she sniffed.

"The city is a growing metropolis, Miss Lawes," Hallie offered, "with a thriving, permanent population." She thought she heard Richard Marksley stifle a laugh.

"I meant society, Miss Ashton. The very best people."

"They are not always so easy to find, Miss Lawes. In such a large and bustling place."

Phoebe's look dismissed the statement; having misunderstood so far, she continued to misinterpret. She, of course, planned to mingle only among the First Circles.

"And when did you last visit London, Miss Ashton?" Squire Lawes inquired.

"Almost two years ago now, sir. To attend services for my cousin Tolliver." Her uncle was not going to aid her in this, though he looked miserable enough. She wished desperately to change the topic.

"Well, we look forward to welcoming him here to Denhurst. No doubt he will be coming to the wedding?"

"Miss Ashton's cousin Tolliver, Mr. Ashton's son, was fatally wounded in France, Squire, at the battle of the Nivelle River." Richard Marksley relayed the information dispassionately, while Hallie breathed her relief. "Tolliver Ashton was an officer with the Light Horse, my old regiment."

"Is that how you met, then?" Phoebe asked, with too eager an interest. "Did Tolliver Ashton introduce you?"

"No, Miss Lawes," he said shortly.

"Oh, I wondered," Phoebe continued lightly, "because Caroline Chalmers had been married about a year by then, yes?"

"Phoebe," Squire Lawes warned. "You will not annoy our guests with such tattle."

Phoebe sat back, but the peevish glance she sent Hallie signaled her intention to persist. Hallie thought the girl immensely foolish; if Phoebe were not careful she would provoke her adored Marksley. Hallie could read his displeasure on his face. But Caroline Chalmers. Who on earth was Caroline Chalmers?

"Ah, the incomparable Caroline Chalmers," Archie Cavendish conveniently supplied. "Now the Dowager Marchioness of Wrethingwell-Drummond. 'She walks in beauty like the night.' 'Tis whispered Byron wrote more than one of his stanzas for her. Saw the Exquisite myself not three months ago. 'A lovelier flower on earth was never sown.' Indeed!"

Richard Marksley eyed Cavendish with what Hallie

could only term weary tolerance. She did not believe that was entirely due to the youth's wild tribute.

"You must be careful, Archibald," the Vicar advised, "to allow for the deficiencies of our party. Not all can spring as swiftly from one reference to another."

"I apologize, ladies and gentlemen," Archibald said. " 'Tis true that my passions lead me to gallop where a more sedate pace would be in order." He brushed a limp lock of blond hair from his no-doubt fevered brow and stared intently at Hallie. "You look to be a sensitive soul, Miss Ashton."

Hallie tried a weak smile.

"I imagine you like poetry," he persisted.

"I . . . yes, I do."

"What are your poetic views, Miss Ashton? Do you place all feeling in the mind, as does Descartes, or—in company with most young ladies," and he shot a pointed glance at Phoebe Lawes, "in the heart?"

Hallie sensed Richard Marksley's close attention.

"I believe the two are inseparable, Mr. Cavendish. Certainly I believe that we love, or hate, as much with the mind as with the heart."

"You are in company with the finest intellects in saying so, Miss Ashton!"

Hallie was less aware of Archie's ardor than of Richard Marksley's quiet regard. She met his gaze, intending to do so only briefly, but found her attention fixed.

"Presumably," he said, "you would never believe in love at first sight then—my dear."

Hallie's chin lifted.

"I do not." She was conscious of all eyes upon her, and felt uncomfortably warm. "Though there may be a certain susceptibility—an inclination. One might wish to love for the mind's reasons, and one's heart then approves the first acceptable candidate."

Squire Lawes laughed. "You must have been *inclined* to Richard here then, Miss Ashton." He laughed again. "And he to you, of course."

But Richard Marksley was looking grim. He had to be recalling her encounter with his cousin Reginald. He would be all too sensitive to the discrepancy between her stated belief and her behavior in that instance.

"What reasons could one have for wishing to fall in love, Miss Ashton?" Archie Cavendish asked. "The poets liken it to a torture of the soul."

"I believe Miss Ashton is confusing love with marriage, Cavendish," Marksley observed dryly. "After all, it is not necessary to be in love to have children."

Hallie blushed as the vicar cleared his throat.

"Are you certain, Mr. Marksley, that that is what you wished to say?"

"I beg pardon, vicar. Unlike Mr. Cavendish, I am not a poet."

"Nevertheless," Squire Lawes proposed with a smile, "I suggest we keep that discussion from this table. We are here to celebrate a betrothal after all." He raised his glass to Hallie and then turned to her uncle.

The discussion at dinner covered the usual speculations concerning fashion, weather, and politics. Were it not for Phoebe Lawes leaning a bit too freely into his arm, and Miss Binkin's unrelenting, glassy attention, Richard felt he might even have relaxed. Mrs. Lawes was a frank woman of common sense and good humor. She liked her horses, dogs, and chickens. She spoke affectionately of Phoebe and her absent younger sons, "the twins." Augusta Lawes was also a competent hostess—capable of carrying a conversation while watching the progress of the meal. She had noticed how often his glance strayed to Harriet Ashton.

"She will make a lovely bride, Richard," she said now, patting his hand. "We are so glad you are settling. 'Tis good to have at least one member of the Marksley family with plans here in Denhurst."

This oblique reference to his cousin's passing acquaintance with Denhurst and his future tenants did not surprise Richard. Reggie's preferences had been all too clear to the good townsfolk for many long years.

"You are too generous, ma'am. I have every reason to stay fixed. You must remember that Denhurst is my home."

"But London is as well, Richard. You have been fair, though, and that is something all of us notice."

The vicar and Phoebe Lawes seconded the comment, while Miss Binkin merely continued to stare. The woman was an oddity.

During a temporary lull in the chatter, Augusta smiled at Hallie. "You seem a very clever young lady, Miss Ashton. I wonder, are you also literary, like Richard?"

"I keep a journal, ma'am," she said, with a swift glance at him. He wondered why she should admit so little with such reluctance. Her shyness, her sudden diffidence, irritated him. He knew she could hold her own in any discussion. But Phoebe interpreted the tight line to his mouth as disapproval.

"One has to be so careful not to be too broody, Miss Ashton. There is always such a danger of becoming a frightful bluestocking." Before either of her frowning parents could reprove her she turned to Richard. "You must have endless submissions at your journal from these busy dabblers, ugly spinsters, no doubt, who want all of us to read every dreary word. But *you* would never care for such trifles, would you, Richard?"

"Miss Lawes, I would not be so particular. There are certain trifles, as you call them, that have appealed to both men and women through the centuries. Certainly if *The Tantalus* were to receive high quality work from ladies, I should like to think we would be keen indeed. 'Twould be an honor to publish such as Anna Seward or Joanna Baillie. To date, however, we have received little."

"And you will not, sir," Alfred Ashton asserted. "Women do not undertake to refine their language. Nor do they have the logical minds required for rational argument. There are simply natural limits that cannot be denied. Even a girl as well read as my niece would be the first to agree to that."

Harriet Ashton did not look as though she agreed with any of it. If eyes alone could be mutinous, Richard deemed that hers were.

"I should not wish to deny the possibility, Mr. Ashton," he said. "I think that every age has its own arrogance. Looking beyond our own time requires a remarkable leap. I might find writing today that I believe will last in appeal for centuries. But I cannot truly know. Similarly, I suspect we are often indifferent, even stubbornly blind, to greatness among us. Fashion, by definition, is fickle and short-lived."

"Oh la, yes," Phoebe Lawes sighed, and fluttered her eyelashes at him.

Archie Cavendish looked excited.

"Are you submitting, sir, that some of those ignored and ridiculed today might a hundred years hence be considered 'great'?"

Richard tried not to smile.

"It is possible, Mr. Cavendish. Although few appear to last more than a generation if they make no impression on their own. But there are always exceptions." This time he did smile. "I have told you I am only enough of a poet to be a critic. All of us have our likes and dislikes, find subjects or phrasing that speak to us and to our experience where another might dismiss them. I imagine everyone at this table has differing preferences as to what is memorable, be it beautiful, haunting, or simply . . . true."

"I say, shall we give it a go?" Archie urged. "Let's hear what people select."

"Oh, Archie, dear," Mrs. Mayhew said, "This is not the time or place for a game. Our hosts—"

"Nonsense, Eleanor," Augusta Lawes exclaimed. "The girls have just removed the pudding. If the gentlemen are willing to forego their cigars and have some port here at the table, I would be most pleased to entertain Archie's experiment."

"Thank you, madam." Magnifying his pale blue eyes by affectedly raising a lorgnette, Archie surveyed the table. "I believe we should begin with the ladies. Perhaps Miss Binkin?"

All gazes sought Millicent Binkin as she turned to Archie, a scowl making her face fierce.

"What am I to do, then?" she asked.

"Why, quote us something you like. Some bit of poetry. Something you have always remembered."

"Young man, I do not clutter my mind with rhymes and other nonsense. It is a distraction from more improving pursuits."

As Archie's face fell, Richard took a sip of port. He had dealt with many of the world's Binkins. Nowadays he rarely troubled himself to persuade them.

"Perhaps," Mrs. Mayhew ventured, "you recall something from your school days, Miss Binkin. Something you memorized for classes."

Miss Binkin frowned at the vicar's wife. Then her brow cleared.

"I do remember something useful. A rule." And she quoted:

Thirty days hath November
April, June, and September
February hath twenty-eight alone
And all the rest have thirty-one.

Phoebe Lawes coughed dramatically, drawing sharp looks from her parents. The rest of the gathering sat mute.

"Most practical, Miss Binkin," Squire Lawes said at last, sending another admonitory glance at his daughter.

"And you've remembered it all this time?" Archie Cavendish asked snidely, still smarting from her earlier dismissal.

Millicent Binkin glared at him. "It has not been all that long, Mr. Cavendish," she snapped. "And this is not much of a game if you are the only one to play it."

"Michael, what do you have for us?" Augusta Lawes asked, turning quickly to the vicar on her left.

"Well, I've a fondness for Cowper," he said with a shy smile. Clearing his throat, he recited in good voice:

God moves in a mysterious way,
His wonders to perform;
He plants his footsteps in the sea,
And rides upon the storm.

"Capital!" Hallie's uncle exclaimed, immediately gratifying the gentle vicar. "I've always liked that as well. Never knew it was Cowper. Thought it was the Bible." As the vicar winced, Augusta Lawes wisely moved ahead.

"Now I must claim my turn, even though I am hostess and should doubtless surrender my spot to someone else. But we do seem to be going 'round the table this direction, after all. I declare this next to be my very favorite. Though you'll think me foolish for failing to recall every word." She pressed a plump hand to her bosom:

> *There is a garden in her face—*
> *Where roses and white lilies blow . . .*

Her rapt expression spoke of her absorption; Richard believed she needed only a moment more before continuing. But Archie Cavendish was unwilling to wait.

"A heavenly paradise is that place, and so on and so on," he finished rudely. "Yes, yes, Campion had a certain panache, but now, don't you know, that business about ripe beauty isn't at all the thing."

Augusta Lawes's stricken gaze sought Richard's. "Oh dear, Richard, is that truly the case? I have always thought it so lovely."

"It is unquestionably lovely, ma'am," Richard assured her. He intended then to direct his attention across the table to Archie Cavendish, but his gaze sought his betrothed. How was he to interpret that look in her eyes? She had no reason to appear as wounded as Augusta Lawes, nor as outraged as he himself felt, yet somehow she managed both.

"Perhaps, Mr. Cavendish," he said to the offender, "you might set an example for the rest of us and carry on? We are loath to try your patience much longer."

The young fool beamed. "Why, of course. I shall be delighted. Ladies and gentlemen, my own selection."

He drew breath, holding it as though preparing to dive, then launched:

Alike as to the fallen snow
A child's pale visage, closed in death
Whispers still of innocence
Lost 'ere it learns to grow!

Oh, mighty unforgiving Death!
To rob us with such awesome skill!
Of love and life, to steal, to kill
With presence undeniable!

As Archie gazed triumphantly around the group, several guests looked down uncomfortably. Others turned toward Richard, though this was a burden he would rather not assume. His teeth had been so tightly clenched that he had difficulty speaking.

"I have not come across this before, Mr. Cavendish."

"It is my own, sir," he boasted. "As yet unpublished."

Richard wondered if the unbridled pup expected him to offer for it. He could not help his troubled frown, or his silence.

"It is most . . . moving, Archie," Augusta Lawes said at last, with greater courtesy than Cavendish had shown to her.

"I think it's terrible," Phoebe said bluntly, her nose in the air. "A dead, cold child! How awful!"

"It is meant to be awful," Archie protested.

"Well, I think you were awful for writing it."

"You have no knowledge of great poetry! Why, you're barely out of the schoolroom!"

"Children," Squire Lawes said mildly, "this squabbling is affecting the digestion. Perhaps we had best stop—"

"Oh no, Papa!" Phoebe cried. "'Tis my turn! And I do know fine poetry." She defiantly tossed her curls as she flounced in her seat and leaned close to Richard. "'Come live with me and be my love,'" she began, with a speed and determination that jarred,

> *And we will all the pleasures prove*
> *That hills and valleys, dales and fields*
> *Woods or sleepy mountain yields.*

"That's *steepy* mountain," Archie corrected loudly.

But Phoebe chose not to hear him. As the girl ogled him, Richard inched away. Phoebe's pert rendering had robbed the lines of any subtlety, of even the faintest hint of invitation. He would never have believed Marlowe could so repel him.

"Lovely, my dear," Augusta Lawes said. "Richard, what do you have for us?" She intended to be kind. But at that moment Richard wanted only for the torturous game to end. And he blamed his discomfort—he blamed the fact that he was here at all—on Hallie Ashton. He stared accusingly across at her.

"'Married in haste, we may repent at leisure.'"

Her cheeks flushed. Was she embarrassed? Good. The whole evening had been an embarrassment.

"Good heavens, Richard, you cannot mean it," Augusta Lawes laughed. "But you are a sly one, are you not? Do not tease us now. You must give us something else. Here is Miss Ashton hoping to hear more romantical stuff."

Romantical? Surely not, with those pale, clenched fists. Miss Ashton looked as though she would have much preferred something martial. Only the eager Phoebe, who was once again pressing her arm against his own, wanted something "romantical." He was in the mood to disoblige her.

" 'If thou be'st borne to strange sights,' " he began slowly, pleased by the recognition in Hallie Ashton's gaze—

> *Things invisible to see*
> *Ride ten thousand days and nights*
> *Till age snow white hairs on thee.*
> *Thou, when thou return'st, will tell me*
> *All strange wonders that befell thee*
> *And swear*
> *Nowhere*
> *Lives a woman*
> *True, and fair.*

He read the silent, angry message from his intended. Then Phoebe Lawes leaned close to whisper, "Caroline

Chalmers truly did break your heart, did she not, Richard?"

His withering glance at least sent the peagoose back to her seat.

"I protest, Richard, these sentiments are not at all the thing," Augusta Lawes lightly tapped him on the arm. "Not at all the thing for an affianced gentleman. You are much too hard, and I fear I shall never forgive you." But her smile robbed the threat of any sting. "Now, Mr. Ashton, perhaps you have some words for us?"

Harriet's uncle muttered something much like a "harrumph!" Richard expected the old goat to refuse to participate, but Ashton surprised him with a firm and forceful:

Breathes there the man with soul so dead
Who never to himself hath said,
'This is my own, my native land'!

He earned applause from the table and the smallest of smiles from Hallie. Richard was gratified to know Alfred Ashton could feel affection for his country, if not for his niece.

"Well done, sir," his host acknowledged. "And now perhaps—Eleanor?"

Mrs. Mayhew demurred. "I cannot hope to contribute anything near as grand as the rest of the company," she said.

"My dear Eleanor," Augusta Lawes advised. "This is not a competition. You simply must say something, for

I know you have a memory for such things so much better than my own."

Mrs. Mayhew smiled sweetly. "Well then, this is from Mr. Coleridge, and I think it rather special:

In Xanadu did Kubla Kahn
A stately pleasure dome decree:
where Alph, the sacred river ran
through caverns measureless to man
down to a sunless sea . . .

She stopped, and modestly covered her lips with one hand.

"Oh, Mrs. Mayhew," Phoebe enthused. "That is so beautiful. Do you not think so, Richard?"

"I do," Richard said with a smile. "And Mr. Coleridge would no doubt thank you for saying so."

"Too fantastical for my taste," Archie Cavendish claimed irreverently. "Everyone knows Coleridge is not quite to rights in his head. Opium eater too, as they say."

Richard looked at him with such severity that the pretentious popinjay actually gaped.

"Perhaps we should draw this to a close then, shall we?" Squire Lawes offered quickly. "We have only to hear from you, Miss Ashton—saving the best for last," he smiled. "You have been observing all of us so quietly. I understand all the young ladies are entranced with Lord Byron. Perhaps you recall some of his verses?"

"I do admire Lord Byron, sir," Hallie said, "but if

you do not object, I should like to respond to Mister Marksley's selection."

"Respond?" The Squire looked amused. "That would be a good bit of work. Had no idea that could be done with this. By all means, m'dear."

Richard watched Hallie Ashton's face, aware of his own expectant tension. What the deuce was the girl up to? Her gaze was steady. It surprised him that he enjoyed the sensation of holding her interest, however defiant.

" 'But true love," she began softly,

> *. . . is a durable fire*
> *In the mind ever burning;*
> *Never sick, never old, never dead,*
> *From itself never turning.*

She could not have been more direct—an ideal of love to counter his own cynical choice. But Richard still had to wonder what she meant by it. Was she in love with Reggie after all? He raised his glass to her.

"I commend you, my dear," he said. "We shall be a family of Elizabethans." It was not what he wanted to say to her; he wanted to tell her she was too clever by half. And he was thinking that she was certainly much too subtle for vain cousin Reggie to comprehend.

"I admire that greatly, Miss Ashton," Archie Cavendish announced. "About another pilgrimage, but unlike Mr. Marksley's Donne, with a faith in love at its close. And your Ralegh addresses whether the head and heart are one. 'True love is a durable fire, in the mind ever burning,' " he repeated. "Splendid!"

The besotted youngster was practically drooling on her sleeve. Despite the fact that Richard actually agreed with Cavendish, as pompous as he sounded, he had to repress the wish to grab him by the cravat and hold hard.

"Oh Papa," Phoebe pleaded, apparently resenting the attention given Hallie Ashton. "We cannot finish until you have said something! All the rest of us have."

"All right then, child. But mind you, you will regret asking me to perform. Let's see, I knew what I intended to say. The only bit I can recite. Here now, and mind your mother's blushes . . .

Of all the girls that are so smart
There's none like pretty Sally
She is the darling of my heart
And she lives in our alley.

The company dispersed in the midst of laughter. Richard thanked his host and Mrs. Lawes, wished the Mayhews well, spared a polite goodnight for the irrepressible Phoebe, and managed to avoid Archie Cavendish's attempts to engage him further. He watched with some satisfaction as the Mayhews drew Archie, protesting, away to their carriage.

As Richard helped Miss Binkin into her seat beside her cousin in the Penham carriage, he noticed Hallie

Ashton kept her face turned from him. He had decided she was definitely deceiving him about her true feelings for Reginald or at the very least about her knowledge of poetry. Recalling their lively discussion while driving on Saturday, he suspected she had some unreasonable fear of being termed, as Phoebe Lawes put it, a blue-stocking.

"I believe you have promised me another drive tomorrow, Miss Ashton," he said, knowing nothing of the sort had been arranged. "I shall plan to be at Penham at three . . . if that is still to your taste?"

A fleeting panic crossed her features. "Oh, but I . . . I fear that will not be possible."

"Why ever not?" Miss Binkin demanded. She turned to Richard. "Miss Ashton and I will be pleased to accompany you, Mr. Marksley."

"Thank you, Miss Binkin," he said, though he had every intention of leaving the dour *duenna* behind. "Until tomorrow, then." And with a low bow he made his own departure.

Chapter Six

Her face must have betrayed her resignation to company. She could think of no other reason for the knowing look with which Richard Marksley greeted her the next afternoon.

"Well met, Miss Ashton," he said, bowing low. "And where is your dedicated shadow, Miss Binkin?"

"Miss Binkin has been invited to tea with the Countess. We shall have a groom to attend us instead."

"Indeed?" Marksley raised an eyebrow. "We would only tolerate surrendering Miss Binkin's bewitching company to the demands of a higher authority." Hallie suspected he had planned the Countess's hasty invitation. When his lips barely restrained a smile, she was certain of it.

For courage, she reminded herself she still had the company of a groom.

"I . . . am ready now, Mr. Marksley."

"At your service, Miss Ashton," he said, offering his arm. "Shall we take some air?"

Her hand rested on his coat sleeve with only the slightest pressure, yet her fingers still trembled against the soft serge.

The day was cool and gray. Lowering clouds highlighted the changing foliage along the drive. A breeze chased leaves across the gravel, leading the horses to toss their heads warily.

"Looks like we be in fer a spot o' weather, sir," the head groom warned Marksley as they crossed to the curricle. A younger groom calmed the skittish team as a sudden gust swirled about their legs.

"We might at that, Tom," Marksley said. He looked down at Hallie. "Would you prefer to delay the outing, Miss Ashton? Tom has an enviable record of forecasting, though I doubt we shall have more than a drizzle within the hour."

Hallie glanced at the spirited horses. They looked as eager for release, for some period of air and motion, as she herself felt.

"If you are amenable to the drive, Mr. Marksley," she said, at last meeting his gaze, "I should like to go out."

She thought his eyes lit briefly in approval. Perhaps he had anticipated her apologies. Any other well-bred young lady would have cried off under similar circumstances. It was never proper to willfully risk one's person or, more particularly, one's wardrobe to the vagaries of the elements. Richard Marksley, whose good manners were so nearly innate, would have known that.

He helped her up onto the seat. As she settled her skirts, he followed and called the young groom to ride behind. Then, with a brief salute from Tom, they were off down the drive at a brisk trot. Hallie checked her bonnet to make certain she would not lose it to the breezes.

"I thought we might head for the river this afternoon," Marksley said. "Squire Lawes seemed to believe the trees along the route to the mill were particularly beautiful this year." His attention settled on her face for some time longer than she found entirely comfortable. As she felt the color mount in her cheeks, she looked away. Of course the groom was riding behind. How absurd of her to forget.

"Did you enjoy the Laweses' dinner last night, Miss Hallie?"

"Yes," she said, reluctantly glancing back at him. "They were pleasant and courteous. And the vicar and Mrs. Mayhew were very kind."

"Their nephew was most generous in his attentions to you, m'dear."

"I found him no more attentive than Squire Lawes, who was also seated beside me."

Richard Marksley smiled, but at the heads of the horses. Hallie found it difficult not to watch his face. She forced her attention away.

"Mr. Cavendish's attempt to enliven the company was most welcome," she said, with more conviction than she felt.

"And his choice of verse?"

"It was, under the circumstances, quite acceptable."

"Ha!" Marksley urged the team to greater speed. "You cannot convince me of that, Hallie Ashton. You were as appalled by that treacle as I was."

"It . . . rhymed," she said, stubbornly seeking refuge once more in falsity. She felt that she might strangle. The world, and Richard Marksley, seemed mad for poetry.

"Oh yes," he agreed grimly, shooting her a considering look, "it rhymed." For a while, negotiating a series of curves, he fell silent. But he was not yet ready to abandon a review of the Laweses' entertainment.

"Miss Lawes has become quite a lively young lady."

Remembering the girl's taunting manner, Hallie clenched her gloved hands.

"Her rendering of Marlowe was certainly *lively*," she agreed.

"You did not care for it?"

"Did you?" she countered.

"I accepted it, Miss Ashton, in the spirit in which it was delivered." When he glanced at her stony expression he added, "Phoebe Lawes is very young."

"She is but two years younger than I, Mr. Marksley."

"You are a woman." For a moment he was silent, then he suggested, "She was likely in a sentimental mood, since the dinner was intended to mark an engagement."

"She may well have been in a 'sentimental mood' as

you term it, sir. But I very much doubt that she recalled the engagement was *ours*."

At that he laughed, an open, relaxed laugh that pleased her. "If I did not know it for an impossibility, Miss Hallie," he said, his dark eyes bright, "I might almost suspect my temporary fiancée of jealousy."

"You would be imagining, sir," she said, looking away. "You are quite thoroughly aware of my views in this matter."

"Am I? I think not. I should like, for one, to receive some instruction from you with regard to Sir Walter Ralegh's meaning. I am familiar with his Walsingham ballad, though not, perhaps, as familiar as your so erudite Mr. Cavendish appears to be. It is usually taken as an affirmation—of love or of fidelity, if you will, despite its misogynous passages. Do I misinterpret, Miss Ashton?"

"As you have noted, sir, the dinner was meant to celebrate our betrothal. I thought your choices unacceptably cynical. You chose to embarrass me, to show your contempt for me quite . . . quite publicly. If the Ralegh recalled you to more gentlemanly behavior I shall consider myself satisfied."

As she finished her voice was unsteady. She dared not look at him for fear that her trembling lips might in fact be a prelude to tears. There was a certain relief in confronting him. The burdens of the past week weighed heavily upon her. But she feared she might only drive him to treat her all the more contemptuously. In her experience, limited though it was, men did not take kindly to any rebuke from a female.

The subsequent silence seemed long, though it could only have lasted a few minutes. They had crossed one bridge over a stream and were approaching another. She could see a mill ahead when Richard Marksley spoke again.

"I owe you an apology, Miss Ashton," he said, his attention pointedly on the ribbons. "Although your reasons for associating with my feckless cousin remain a mystery to me, I have never known you to act with anything less than propriety. In such light, my treatment of you has indeed been ungentlemanly." He paused, then turned to her. "You have given me every indication that you find our plight as unwelcome as I do. I have been unforgivably rude."

His gaze held such intensity that Hallie was drawn to respond. His pride in his own judgment, in his own fairness, had clearly been set back. His sincerity served to provoke her own. She would be as honest and tell him the truth.

"Mr. Marksley . . . Richard, I . . . Oh!" The curricle lurched, a hard jolt that tilted the vehicle immediately and dangerously to the side. Hallie slid abruptly against Richard Marksley's arm, an arm as hard as iron as he fought to control the frightened team. Hallie grabbed for the rail behind the seat and tried to pull herself away from him. As she did so she noticed the groom had been tossed to the roadway, and now sat sprawled in the dirt.

"Are you hurt, lad?" Marksley called to him.

The boy looked dazed, but shook his head.

"See if you can take their heads, then. I must help Miss Ashton down."

The boy quickly leapt to his feet.

"'Tis the wheel what's broke, sir," he gasped as he took the horses' mouths. "Cracked right through it is."

"Deuce take it," Marksley muttered. He eased himself carefully from the high bench to stand in the road. "Miss Ashton," he said, raising his arms toward her. "If you will."

Hallie inched along the skewed seat back, only to determine that there was no choice but to slide in an ungainly manner across the bench toward him. Once having made that move, she slipped easily off the vehicle and into Richard Marksley's waiting arms.

He caught the momentum of her slide, for a brief moment clasping her to him. She could feel the length of him through her clothing. Then he was carefully putting her away from him.

"I hope you have survived intact, Miss Ashton."

"Yes." She avoided his gaze. "Yes, I am fine. Just startled."

"Indeed. I have lost wheels before, but one usually has some warning." He looked at the fractured wheel, several spokes awry and the wood rim splintered. "We were devilishly lucky. You might have been tossed from the seat as well."

It was starting to rain. Hallie noticed the first few darker drops against the shoulders of Marksley's coat before she felt them herself. For a moment, she tilted her face to the fresh sprinkles, only to open her eyes to Richard Marksley's perusal.

"We'd best take shelter in the mill," he said. She thought he looked apologetic, as though he believed her so impressionable as to wish to experience a downpour.

He turned with determination to the groom. "Help me release the horses," he said to him, moving quickly to the front of the curricle. "You must ride Balius and trail Xanthus. Rub them down well when you get back. There's a good lad."

Hallie moved unbidden toward the mill. The shower had strengthened. As she felt water drip from her bonnet down into her collar, she raised her skirts and ran.

The old mill was dry, if not warm. From the outside it had appeared inhabited, but once through the door the unmistakable signs of neglect were everywhere. Hallie moved across a dusty, shuttered parlor to a back room that faced the river. Through dingy glass panes she could see that the rain was now heavy enough to disturb the surface of the water. Even the hills beyond were partially obscured by low clouds. For some time she lost herself in contemplating such an excess of gray in land and sky.

"I have sent the groom back for the carriage," Marksley said as he came into the room. Then he seemed to notice her thoughtful regard for their surroundings. He ran one finger along a dusty table edge and examined the residue with lifted brows. "Haskell abandoned the place some years ago. I had no idea it was such a shambles."

"From the outside it has . . . presence," Hallie said. Her gaze returned to the rain-pocked river and the subdued foliage along the shore. "Indeed, it could not have been sited with greater mastery, just here at river's bend, with veiled hills sleeping at lee, and these pensive oaks to attend." When she turned to him, she would have said more. But the arrested look on his face forestalled further comment. For a moment she met his dark gaze, then she glanced distractedly back at the river. She frowned as she tried to recall what she had said—what slip she must have made—to have silenced him so thoroughly.

"Beauty does not often bear dissection," he said at last. He had moved closer. "As we see, the mill is now little more than a storehouse, and a dusty one at that. The first impression may indeed be charming, but close inspection yields," he blew the dust from his glove, "fairy powder."

She smiled. "I cannot credit such an opinion to you, sir. Where would all of your authors be without discoursing on beauty? You would deprive them of a favorite subject."

"Assuredly. Which is why their editor must cling to whatever cold reason prevails." When he smiled back Hallie's breath caught in her throat. She had been fighting the attraction he held for her. Somehow, in the close confines of this dim and musty room, that smile was a beacon.

"Surely," he said, holding her gaze as he moved toward her, "you have something germane to quote me on the subject? Given the ease with which you riposted last night, you have the poets of the ages at your command." His voice coaxed, but the expression in his eyes held enough of a challenge to force Hallie's own gaze away.

"You grant me too ready a wit, sir." The air seemed not only stale, but stifling. "I said the one thing that came to mind."

That he disbelieved her was evident from his silence—and from the betraying rhythm of Hallie's own duplicitous heart. Yet he would not move away.

The rain gathered force, drumming on the old shingle roof, stinging the surface of the river.

" 'For where is any author in the world,' " he quoted softly, " 'teaches such beauty as a woman's eye?' " His gloved hand moved to turn her face to his. "It intrigues me," he said, as his thumb moved lightly against her chin, "how some part of you always seems to be dreaming. It's in your eyes. Even now." His gaze would not permit her to hide. "What are you dreaming about, my dear?"

He asked so softly that at first Hallie believed she had not heard him correctly. She could catch the scent of his skin and of his rain-dampened wool coat. As close as he was, heaven help her, she wanted him that much closer.

"The groom—"

"Should be halfway to Penham by now. Where he will dutifully report to Miss Binkin." Marksley smiled, then startled her by asking, "Did Reggie kiss you?"

Hallie answered with a proud tilt of her chin.

"Did he kiss you?" Marksley repeated softly.

"Yes . . . But he was—"

"So you have been kissed before."

Before? She watched his lips, which seemed so unaccountably close. Some small, still thinking part of her protested that no, she had never been kissed before.

He bent his head. Her lips caught his breath. She was scarcely aware of her own action in moving to press her open palms against the lapels of his coat. But he must have thought she intended to push him away.

To her dismay he stepped back too many inches. As Hallie looked at her betraying hands, she knew his gaze was on her still. Now was the time to tell him.

"There is something," she began, "something that you must know."

"About Reginald?" he asked, and his gaze hardened.

"Not precisely. Although he is the reason—" Footsteps in the parlor beyond sounded loud in the empty building, immediately silencing her.

"Well, dash it all," Archie Cavendish's supercilious voice was unmistakable, "They seem to have vanished, if they were ever—ah!"

He stopped abruptly in the doorway, so abruptly that Phoebe Lawes, following close behind him, collided with his back. But Hallie thought Phoebe's pout and narrowed gaze had less to do with any affront to her dignity than to the sight of Richard Marksley standing so very close to Hallie.

She could sense the sudden tension in him, as though he would shield her.

"Cavendish," he acknowledged. "Miss Lawes. Have you also sought shelter from the storm?" Both Archie and Phoebe looked scarcely damp.

"Your groom informed us of your um . . . mishap," Cavendish said. He raised a quizzing glass to observe the two of them with relish. "As we have Squire Lawes's carriage, we thought we might offer to take you up, and thus spare you any further . . . inconvenience." He simpered. "That is, if you would like to return to Penham now?"

"Good heavens, Richard," Phoebe said familiarly, stepping into the room with a handkerchief to her nose. "What a filthy place to stop. I wonder you could bear it." Her look dismissed Hallie before she moved to Marksley's side and casually laid her hand on one taut sleeve. "Do come with us now. Papa's carriage is so delightfully appointed. I trust you will tell little difference between it and the Earl's." Her laugh was forced as she started to urge him toward the doorway. "Do come."

But Marksley turned to Hallie.

"It would be best, Miss Ashton," he said. "We should not keep their horses standing in the rain."

She felt oddly forlorn. And she was conscious of Phoebe's open interest that her intended should sound so very formal. He should have called her Hallie just now, especially now, when they had been so very close.

"Come, Miss Ashton," Cavendish added, "You can

only wish to vacate this hole." Hallie walked toward the doorway. She did not care for the look in Archie Cavendish's eyes; what little imagination he possessed had attributed to her the most wanton behavior. He had caught them in a delicate situation. But surely that was not so startling for a betrothed couple?

Hallie refused his arm. They walked ahead of Phoebe and Marksley, pausing only to draw their cloaks about them before racing the rain to the carriage.

Joining Phoebe's waiting maid, the ladies took the seats facing forward. As Archie was directly across from her, Hallie had to turn her head to catch Richard Marksley's expression. She was aware of him, however. Aware of his silence and of the occasional glance he sent to her corner. She anticipated his looks, and managed to stare steadily out the window when they came.

Phoebe leaned forward to gaze appealingly at Marksley. "The mill is in a dreadful state, do you not think so, Richard?"

" 'Tis not congenial, Miss Lawes," he agreed, "though Haskell worked hard in his time. I shall make inquiries. Perhaps there has been some trouble in the family. The property is a fine one. Even if a working mill is no longer viable, the place should be tended."

"Perhaps," Archie suggested, with a mischievous look at Hallie, "the mill should be left as it is. It seems suitable for more *unrefined* purposes. Trysting, for example."

Marksley sent him an icy glance, then turned to the window. "I hope the weather will improve by the morrow," he said. "I have business in London. I shouldn't care for the journey," he added grimly, "with the roads so impassable."

"But Richard," Phoebe cried. "Whatever can you mean by this? When you are to be wed in two weeks' time!"

"Miss Ashton knows that my responsibilities will not cease upon our marriage. Indeed," and Hallie caught his look, "they can only increase."

"Well, there are a good many events you shall miss, and not a few of them planned in your honor." Phoebe's tone was aggrieved. She had anticipated the social whirl. But her subsequent look at Hallie was considering. "Whatever shall you do without him, Miss Harriet? Or will you enjoy the escort of some of the other gentlemen of Denhurst?"

Hallie tried to believe the girl had not meant to impugn her morals. "You flatter me, Miss Lawes. My uncle will no doubt ensure that the next fortnight's entertainments will not be too diverting."

Richard Marksley acknowledged that likelihood with a contemptuous little breath.

"I would be happy to serve as your escort in Mr. Marksley's absence, Miss Ashton," Archie offered. "That is, for the next few days. And with your permission, sir." He tilted his head toward the aloof man next to him. Hallie credited Marksley's expression to the distaste he felt for any reminder of their impending wedding.

"Miss Ashton is free to do as she chooses," he said, "now, three weeks, or even three years hence."

Cavendish stared. "That is remarkably liberal thinking, I must say, sir. Though I should not be surprised, given the views in our intellectual circles. Mary Wollstonecraft's contrary writings are much discussed, are they not? And it is said that Lord Byron believes—"

"I honor the institution of marriage, and the sanctity of marriage vows, Mr. Cavendish," Marksley said coldly. "You mistook my meaning."

"Pardon me, sir. But this talk of freedom for a wife—"

"I hold that spouses should be equal partners in spirit, in the accommodation of each other's wishes, even if not deemed so in the letter of the law."

Phoebe leaned forward again and playfully tapped Richard Marksley on one knee. He shifted his leg away.

"That is so very romantic, Richard. Although," and she lowered her gaze with belated modesty, "I should have expected such from you."

"And do you share Mr. Marksley's romantic views, Miss Ashton?" Cavendish asked, leaning toward her.

"Naturally Mr. Marksley and I have reached a certain understanding of each other's wishes," she replied carefully. "You might consider it 'romantic' that our understanding is confidential. I believe such *privacy*," she stressed, "is key to any true meaning of the word."

Apparently deaf to her reprimand, Cavendish gazed admiringly at her, but Phoebe looked as though Hallie had suddenly started to speak Chinese.

"Miss Ashton is impressively logical," Marksley remarked evenly, with a glance that was unreadable. "Logic is rarely paired with romance."

"Miss Ashton is all that is charming," Archie enthused. Hallie felt him press the toe of his boot against the hem of her skirt. She shot him a look of angry amazement, and attempted to regain her hem, but the young man was persistent.

"Our love is our bond," he cried. "Not for the faint-hearted, no! But proved beyond doubt, through fire and snow!"

After a moment's silence, Marksley said, "That is most amusing doggerel, Mr. Cavendish." His tone was as haughty as Hallie had heard from him. "Where ever did you hear it?"

Archie looked crestfallen, but having had her fill of him, Hallie was grateful for the snub.

"Oh, never mind, Archie," Phoebe said impatiently. "It is not so very awful, but you really must stop imposing on Richard." The comment did very little to restore good will amongst the occupants of the carriage.

The ride continued in shared discomfort. The roads were uneven due to the rain, which pummeled the carriage roof in ceaseless accompaniment to the splashing of the horses' hooves. As they at last pulled to the front of Penham Hall, the rain became a deluge.

"I beg your pardon, Miss Lawes, Mr. Cavendish, if I

do not suggest you stop with us." Marksley was pushing open the door even as he spoke. "In this flood, you are no doubt eager to reach home. We are most grateful for your consideration. Another time, perhaps?"

Indecision and frustration warred on Phoebe's face. "Why I . . . no doubt you are right, Richard. Mama will be worried. I had best be home for tea. And Archie must ready himself. He departs Saturday for Oxford."

"Ah, do you, sir?" Marksley extended his hand. "Until next time then. Miss Ashton, I believe we must risk the damp." He transferred his hand to hers and pulled her none too gently out of the carriage. Two footmen, looking bedraggled, waited with umbrellas at the bottom of the steps. Hallie murmured her thanks to Phoebe Lawes before the carriage door shut with alacrity behind her.

Burdened by her heavy skirts, she had difficulty matching Marksley's pace up the steps to the door. But she arrived close beside him nonetheless, to see Lady Penham's tear-streaked face and hear her anguished moan. She waved a sheet of paper in front of them.

"Richard, Richard! He is dead! My darling boy is dead!"

Chapter Seven

Richard heard Hoskins' soft "milord" as the Penham butler removed his wet coat. He had heard Geneve's wail as well, but he would not quite have believed it without the butler's instant and ominous confirmation.

He reached for his aunt's shoulders and the shaking letter at the same time, holding the grieving woman steadily while he scanned the message. But it was Hallie Ashton to whom he looked.

"It seems my cousin's quest was successful," he told her flatly. "He found an excellent hunter—who helped him break his neck."

Geneve shook beneath his arm as she wept, but Richard could not seem to look away from Hallie Ashton's face. *Tell me what you are thinking,* he found himself demanding silently, *tell me what he meant to you.* Apart from shock at the unexpected news, Richard could read nothing more in her gaze than compassion for Geneve.

"Come, aunt," he said, taking Geneve's hands in one of his. "You must sit down at once. Miss Ashton, please be good enough to join us."

She still looked troubled but composed. Or was she secretly suffering? Could it be that her heart was breaking? He frowned as he led his aunt into the drawing room and settled her by the fire. Then he turned to pour them a brandy.

"It is impossible," Geneve cried. "I cannot believe it. Richard, there must be some mistake. You must send to Ireland at once and ask for the truth of it. They must have made a mistake."

Richard sighed. "There is no mistake. This is uncle's agent in Kildare. I had written him to locate Reggie. The good man has taken it upon himself . . . that is, he has already arranged for Reggie's return. I am sorry."

Geneve wrung her hands. "But he . . . you . . . oh, this cannot be!"

"My lady," Hallie Ashton said softly. "You have had a shock. You will need time—"

Geneve turned on her almost savagely. "None of this is your concern now, miss. You can know nothing of my . . . of our grief."

Richard's lips firmed. "You are undoubtedly distraught, madam. But you forget yourself." He had noticed Hallie Ashton's pallor and suggested she take a seat as well. Still damp from their earlier carriage accident, they both could have benefited from hot baths and a change of clothing. But the fire would have to suffice for the moment. He remained standing stiffly at the hearth.

"Have you told uncle?" he asked.

"The steward, that Mr. . . . Mr. . . ."

"Appleby," Richard supplied.

". . . was to go up to him," Geneve said. "I simply could not. Ah, I fear this will be the end of him! Our own dear boy! Dear Reginald!" She bowed her head as her body trembled.

Hallie Ashton sat quietly, her hands clasped in her lap. Given the rejection of her earlier offer of sympathy, her silence was understandable, but Richard had expected something else . . . that she should need comfort as well. What inanity—to presume that she should need him!

He directed his attention to Geneve.

"My dear aunt," he told her, "I cannot console you. But I can assure you that I would never have wished this."

Her watery blue gaze focused on his face. "He was born and bred to this, Richard. It was his birthright. And now you . . . well," she dabbed at her eyes with a linen square. "It is impossible that he is gone. That you should replace him. All this—to you! We must hope you can make do."

"I shall endeavor to be worthy." He might have pointed out to her that he was more "born and bred" to this than his departed cousin. But Geneve would believe what she would; mere facts had never hindered her assumptions. And Hallie Ashton had no need to know of his parents' unfortunate history. He certainly felt no pressing desire to enlighten her. There was, however, another matter that begged to be addressed. He had considered it immediately, and with grim purpose.

"The marriage must go forward," he said.

Geneve looked up and fixed him with accusing, red-rimmed eyes. "This is not a time to jest, Richard."

He let his gaze survey Hallie Ashton's rebellious features before he responded. "I am quite serious, ma'am. Although it comes so soon after Reggie's passing, a wedding must not be put off. There is now no reason for delay, and no choice."

"And why, sir," Geneve demanded, "do you say so? It is appalling to contemplate a wedding. And to contract a union with this—with such as Miss Ashton *now* is outside of enough. Why, were you to do so now, people would only believe you *had* to marry. I should shudder to be seen in society! Such a misalliance. It is unseemly!" She turned to the tight-lipped Miss Ashton. "I am certain you must agree, Miss Ashton. A future Earl must look much higher. It is your obligation to society, to your family, to step aside now and let him—"

"My dear aunt," Richard interrupted. "You did not appear to find the circumstances unseemly this past week. I remind you that even then I was a member of this family. I regret my cousin's demise in more ways than you can imagine. But the misfortune cannot alter my purpose in this. We must simply beg your forbearance in suffering the association."

Geneve began to weep. "But . . . we would all be wearing mourning."

"Which would be only too appropriate. I do not propose a celebration, aunt. While our state of mourning is regrettable, it is not prohibitive. We cannot wait six months—or even one."

"Too cruel, Richard! Have you no sense of decorum, no delicacy, no sympathy? No thought of what is owed to those who raised you?"

"Remember your promise," he reminded her darkly.

Geneve drew a ragged breath, but pressed on, her hands nervously working the linen of her kerchief.

" 'Tis not as though you were ever obligated since it was Reginald after all who compromised the girl."

"The truth of that is unmistakable. But as the argument did not signify when I made it last week, it cannot signify now."

"I never thought you vengeful, Richard."

"I am not vengeful, aunt. This is not a matter of vengeance. It is quite clearly one of honor. It did not matter much before. Indeed, it had certain farcical aspects," he shot a glance at Hallie, whose color was rising, "but it matters a great deal now. What would you have said of the family? Reggie may have compromised Miss Ashton before, but I have compromised her since."

Hallie Ashton's complexion now warmed radically. Richard could not have explained his satisfaction in the effect. But his attention returned abruptly to Geneve's wide eyes.

"You need not look so horrified, madam," he told

her. "We have done nothing unwonted. We have merely acted the parts you directed us to play, as an affianced couple. But if I were to cry off now, Miss Ashton would most certainly face disgrace. Her uncle would have every right to sue for breach."

Geneve turned her furious attention to Hallie Ashton. "I have no doubt, miss," she hissed, "that this has all been your doing. That you set your cap for my darling boy and drove him—drove him!—to his death. He would not have gone to Ireland at all had you not imposed yourself! And now you will cling to Richard and drag us all down into the gutter. Oh—that Cyril's heir should so condescend! Such a woman as you are! I know not what to call you. You will forever be no more than dirt in my eyes, you . . . you—"

"Enough," Richard snapped. "Miss Ashton will shortly belong to this family, as the Viscountess Langsford, and as such you will treat her with civility." Hallie Ashton had the misfortune at that moment to sneeze, which reminded him that they both needed dry clothing. "You know full well, aunt, that nothing you have said has any merit whatever. I shall try to understand. You have suffered a terrible loss. You are in shock. Your judgment is unsound. But have a care." He glanced again at Hallie Ashton's face. "And now, if you will excuse us, we suffered a carriage accident this afternoon. If Miss Ashton is not immediately attended to, she might well fall ill."

Geneve's glare expressed her unspoken desire for that very eventuality, or worse. She rose with an exaggerated swish of her elegant silk skirts, although her flushed, ravaged features robbed the display of the dignity she would have wished.

"I shall not argue, Richard. You know I disapprove. Forgive me if I leave your wedding plans in your eager hands. I shall find arrangements for the funeral of *my son* to be trying enough. But I shall never forgive you, Richard. I know you do this to spite me."

"No, ma'am," Richard said as pleasantly as he could. He made her a slight bow. "I do this in spite of you. There is a world of difference."

With a toss of her head and another bitter glance at Hallie Ashton, Geneve left them together.

"I . . . feel for her," Hallie Ashton said. "She must be suffering."

"Your sympathy does you credit, my dear. But let me promise you that she will pull through. I have known her many years."

"Still . . . with such a shock—"

He smiled grimly as he examined her. "I assure you that she lacks your sensitivity. I apologize for anything she may have said that offended you."

"She cannot offend me."

"Cannot? Brave words, Miss Hallie. The countess has offended me on innumerable occasions."

Hallie Ashton rose to her feet and attempted to smooth out her wrinkled skirt. "Then you must have cared more than you own . . . and tried to please her."

Richard eyed her thoughtfully. "You are remarkably wise, my dear. For such an innocent." Her flush deepened. "But I see now that I have offended you." He smiled, but she did not take up his challenge.

"The wisdom you commend, Mr. Marksley, was Tolly's. He thought it a waste to spend one's life attempting to please another. Perhaps he learned early that my uncle cannot be pleased. Neither did he believe in unmet expectation—in living on dreams alone. Tolly was always one for making his own way."

Tolliver Ashton, by Jeremy's report, had lived as he thought—as a young man of purpose and action.

"Then I drink to the wise philosophy of your late cousin Tolly," he said, toasting Hallie Ashton before letting the brandy warm his throat and chest. "Do you feel nothing at all then?" he quizzed her.

"I . . . do not understand you."

"Do you feel nothing upon the death of my own cousin?" He watched her very closely. "Your dear one will not be visiting anyone ever again. You expectation of his return," he paused, "will never be gratified."

"I have told you before. He was never dear to me."

"What attraction did he hold for you, then?" Despite his best effort he knew his voice betrayed his frustration. "What did he have that you could possibly have wanted?"

"Nothing. Nothing but a name."

"A name? I see." His lips firmed. "I see that my aunt comprehends you."

"No. She does not."

"How very cryptic, Miss Ashton. Given your fondness for apt sayings, one might accuse you of purposely speaking in some peculiar code of your own." To his surprise, she smiled. A shy, secretive smile that, to his irritation, fascinated him.

"You had best see to your warmth," he said sharply, turning from her to place the brandy snifter carefully on the mantel. "No matter the circumstances, my aunt is punctilious about the dinner hour. Though it seems unlikely she will desire it, I would prefer that she have our company." But when he turned, prepared to acknowledge Hallie Ashton's relieved departure, he found her instead observing him with some concern.

"Is it possible, my lord, that you feel more in this instance than you would have anyone know?"

"Indeed I do, Miss Ashton. But my feelings are all entirely selfish—and have much to do with your very proper use of 'my lord,' as you said it just now."

"It is . . . expected."

"Yes." And then, because she still stood there, and perhaps because the brandy had loosened his tongue, he said, "Much as I disdained him, my dear departed cousin served one very useful function. He was the Viscount Langsford, heir to the Earl of Penham, and I, within limits, could do as I chose." He turned back to the mantel and idly ran a finger along its edge.

"But Jeremy—forgive me—Lord Jeremy told me that your own father was once the Viscount Langsford."

He turned to her in surprise. "That is true, yes. But my father lost the title before I was born. I have never regretted it nor anticipated its restoration." He paused.

"Jeremy is perhaps too familiar with family histories. And too free with mine."

"Yet you would have me be part of it. That is, if you are serious."

"Oh, I am serious, Miss Ashton. We no longer have an option. The two of us shall spend the rest of our days paying for the transgressions of a selfish boy, one who was denied nothing in life . . . except its continuance."

Hallie Ashton shivered, whether with dread at the prospect or not, Richard could not have said. He had, he realized, actually been enjoying her company. But now, with Reggie's death and the burdens ahead, sparring with her no longer afforded an amusing, if strangely strained, game. The situation was now quite suffocatingly serious. She had best be aware of that fact.

"You are cold," he said. "You should retire."

"Yes, only . . . Is it true, then? That you do truly believe marriage is our only course?"

"Of a certainty, my dear. Unless another suitor lays claim to your affections?" As she slowly shook her head, he added, "Reggie was to be our savior. I fear no additional eager prospects have presented themselves. And you and your uncle deserve more than mere purchase."

At that she blanched, which made him feel a brute.

"You will find that a good reputation does matter in life, Miss Hallie. More so, unfairly so, perhaps, for a young lady. But preserving one's good name provides a measure of freedom as well—that is, if one has any intention of living as anything other than a hermit. I cannot pretend it is an optimal arrangement, but, speaking from my relatively lofty experience, it can prove sufficient."

She took a step closer to him. "I am sorry that this has happened, my lord. I am sorry that my . . . my actions have led to your distress."

"Distress?" He raised an eyebrow as he watched her face, so close to his own. "I am not in distress, Miss Hallie. I am too numb."

"I suspect that is the brandy talking, my lord."

"And now you are already sounding like a wife."

She looked as though he had slapped her. Then she wheeled to flee the room. As he watched her retreating figure, he had the bittersweet satisfaction of knowing that he had at last offended her.

"The devil," he muttered, and contemplated the fire.

She had come too close, seen too much. Reggie had made his youth a misery, his antics had threatened to plague Richard into his dotage, yet he would never have wished his cousin dead. He was long past envy of Geneve's excessive affection for her own. No, what he felt was sadness at the waste of a life, and the abrupt end of promise.

But it was also true that a heavy dose of self-pity was affecting him. He was not at all certain he would be able to maintain his dedication to *The Tantalus*, at least not to the former degree. He was fond of his work—his little hobby, as Geneve termed it. And a nagging mystery, the unresolved business with Henry Beecham, was vastly troubling. He had to accept that he might never meet that particular gentleman. Beecham might have to find another sponsor. And Richard would be left with a lingering dissatisfaction, the result of an unfulfilled quest. What had she termed it? Expectation never gratified. Indeed.

There was something else he had scarcely dared admit: that beyond his stated purpose in forwarding the wedding, something had taken root in him that was curiously possessive, something he was not at all certain he liked and that certainly was not comfortable or soothing. He had felt it at the mill, he felt it now—a fierce determination to wed Hallie Ashton, as a means to remove her from her despot of an uncle, and to erase any memory of Reggie.

Staring at the flames he resolved to direct his steps to London immediately after the funeral. He had much to arrange. And it was best to leave her.

Reginald Falsworth Marksley's funeral took place three days later in the village church he had not visited for years. The mourners accompanied his remains to the Penham plot, listened dutifully to Vicar Mayhew's service, and subsequently stayed to offer their condolences to the family. The Earl of Penham did not attend his own son's funeral, being himself bedridden and, some said, too sickly to recognize fully the enormity of his loss.

Hallie had carefully avoided Richard Marksley's company after their interview in the drawing room, and he, in any event, was busy helping his aunt prepare for the funeral. The day after its observance he had departed, as scheduled, for London. Hallie could only assume he was planning their nuptials. Certainly no one else, not her uncle, not the Countess, not Miss Binkin nor Hallie herself, had given any thought to the demands of another ceremony. The new Viscount Langsford would handle all the niceties. This wedding was in all ways, she thought, a travesty—a painful mingling of tragedy and burlesque.

The skies did not clear. Hallie spent most of her time in the library, where she could escape her uncle and Millicent. The Countess retired for much of each day to her own rooms where, one could only assume, she wept. Alfred Ashton ventured out every morning to shoot at any living creature that dared show itself on the Earl's estate. At meals, conversation was absent or desultory. After dinner, Hallie played the pianoforte in the parlor, though the effort was for her ears alone.

In such relative solitude she was again able to read and to write in her journal. She applied herself once more to that persistently teasing notion of a poem, the birth of which promised to ease an unaccountable anxiety. She occasionally watched the front drive from the library windows for any sign of a messenger or of Jeremy's return. The sooner she heard that Jeremy had successfully located George Partridge, the better.

She moved away from the window and once again took a seat by the library fire. The servants at Penham, now familiar with her habits, prepared the blaze early each morning. Only Miss Binkin dared interrupt the quiet, but she never stayed long, claiming as she did that the library was too dark and drafty for her joints. Hallie did not find the room chilly, though she knew that her reception of her cousin was markedly so.

If only he would come!

She meant Marksley, not Jeremy, and with the realization, she frowned.

She had wanted to meet Marksley, to have him know her. The letters had not been enough. It had been natural to want to meet the man. But having met him, it had perhaps not been entirely natural to want more. She remembered how he had helped her from the carriage at the mill, the momentary shock and thrill of being clasped to him, the certainty that he had been so very close to kissing her. Indeed, his gaze alone had kissed her.

When the butler knocked on the library door and entered with a letter on a tray, Hallie glanced at him guiltily, aware of her improper thoughts. For a confused second she anticipated something for Beecham from Marksley. But the note was from Jeremy:

Dearest Hallie,

You must be wondering what has become of me. The bird has proved difficult to flush; perhaps I am not as skilled a hunter as you require. I have seen enough of the country now, from Worcester to Wilts., to sustain me for many seasons. Never again doubt my dedication to your cause.

My search has brought me full circle. I have tracked the wandering partridge to a region neighboring your own, whence it should be that much easier to reach you once I am successful. Let us hope you understand me, that you maintain your good spirits, and that friend Richard has shown you all due respect and honor. I have every intention of seeing you shortly, certainly before your anticipated nuptials.

I remain as ever, yours in friendship,

Jeremy Asquith

Hallie read the message several times. It was dated only that morning. Jeremy might well return by the weekend. And she would have to be ready to leave—to catch a mail coach to Portsmouth and purchase passage.

She folded the note, then tucked it into her journal. Perhaps she could ride to Denhurst, there to hire a chaise to the nearest posting inn. Even her uncle might be relied upon to supply her, unknowingly, with information as to means. At this late stage, he would never suspect where her inquiries tended.

Yet even as she adhered to her plans, Hallie knew she had little will to realize them. She had thought she could not impose herself on a man who did not love her, on a man so beholden to honor. But surely there were worse situations.

Hoskins interrupted her reverie once more to inform her that Mrs. Lawes and her daughter had come to call. As the countess was indisposed, he asked whether Miss Ashton would care to receive them.

Hallie agreed, rallying to her obligation. Mrs. Lawes had been kind and Phoebe could be endured. She joined them in the drawing room, where Augusta Lawes's cheery greeting met her at the door.

"Miss Ashton, how delightful to see you again! Whatever have you been doing with yourself in all this dreadful weather?"

"I have been biding my time in the library, ma'am," Hallie said with a smile.

Phoebe raised her pert little nose.

"How dull you must find it!" She sniffed, moving to a side table to examine a miniature portrait of Reginald Marksley.

"It is in truth quite stimulating, Miss Lawes. There is a fine volume of Marlowe." That drew Phoebe's startled attention, but Hallie merely smiled again and moved to the sofa. "It is most kind of you to call," she said, letting Augusta Lawes take the seat beside her. "These have been unhappy times here at Penham. But I did enjoy your dinner last week. What news have you of your other guests? I understand Mr. Cavendish has gone up to Oxford?"

"Oh yes. Dear Archie. The Mayhews sorely miss the lad, I assure you. Though lately he has tended to be a bit listless and out-of-sorts. Eleanor Mayhew even feared he might have a brain disorder. But Michael assured her such was not the case."

"I am . . . glad to hear it."

"That was a moving service Michael Mayhew gave for Lord Reginald, did you not think so, Miss Ashton?"

"Yes indeed."

"Did you ever meet Richard's cousin, Miss Ashton?" Phoebe asked. She had abandoned the portrait, and now fingered a porcelain figurine on a side table. "He was most handsome. But apart from that, he and Richard were not at all alike."

"I . . . never had the pleasure of meeting the Viscount Langsford," Hallie lied.

"But now you plan to marry the Viscount Langsford," Phoebe suggested slyly. "How long must you postpone the wedding?"

"We do not intend to postpone it," Hallie said. "In fact, Mr.—Lord Langsford is most determined that we not change our plans."

Phoebe's eyebrows rose as Mrs. Lawes exclaimed, "My dear, how surprising! Surely the family are all in mourning?"

"I believe the Countess does indeed find the situation difficult. But the Viscount believes it for the best."

"Well, of course, it is his choice." Augusta affirmed. "And he is a most sensible young man."

"Oh, certainly," Phoebe added. "I understand the gentlemen are often eager to marry or feel a certain . . . necessity." Her mother pursed her lips, but Phoebe ignored her. "Will you marry in Denhurst?"

"I believe so," Hallie said. "Once the Viscount returns from London. Possibly as soon as next week."

Phoebe at once looked dejected. Perhaps she had not anticipated that her needling would elicit information that was quite so unpalatable. *But you may have him after all,* Hallie assured her silently, wondering why the thought made her feel so wretched.

"We shall certainly wish you both the best," Augusta

Lawes said with a pointed look at her daughter, "won't we Phoebe? And I know Squire Lawes would join me in saying so."

"You are too kind, ma'am. And how is Squire Lawes?"

"Tolerable, my dear, tolerable. But having these gypsies wander into the county has caused him a great deal of bother. Have you not heard?" she asked, meeting Hallie's inquiring gaze.

"No. They have camped near Denhurst?"

Augusta Lawes nodded. "No more than a few miles out, which is as good as traipsing into town! We all know what gypsies mean."

"It is exciting!" Phoebe gushed. "The men are all so dark and romantic, and the women dance and tell fortunes. I do wish the weather would clear. We could make a picnic out by the gypsy caravans and have our fortunes told."

Augusta Lawes clucked. "And have your purses stolen! No, Phoebe, you should not wish for such a thing."

Hallie turned to Augusta. "What is it that concerns your husband, ma'am?"

"He serves as magistrate, as you know, my dear. It was his duty to warn the troupe not to cause trouble. Three years ago there was a kidnapping."

"A kidnapping!" Phoebe exclaimed. "Mama! I never heard!"

"Little Arthur Wells, my dear. The twins' playmate from Budgely Academy. But he was found to have visited a young friend, and not to have been with the gypsies at all."

"And yet, ma'am," Hallie said. "You believe the gypsies were responsible?"

"How could they not be? For he never would have wondered off had he not been enticed by example. Those roving gypsy ways! Arthur was always a most dutiful little boy."

Hallie refrained from comment. "How likely are the gypsies to stay, Mrs. Lawes?" she asked instead.

"Not long, my dear, if the Squire has his way. Though they will want to have their circuses or whatever before departing."

"I should dearly love to see the circus," Phoebe said, with a toss of her plump curls. "I believe I shall go even if Papa forbids it."

Her mother looked at her in exasperation. "I do not understand you, Phoebe. There is nothing at all mysterious about these people. They live a poor, coarse, and unsettled life. Prophecies and fortunes! You must not disobey your father."

"But Mama, you were just reading *Guy Mannering* the other night!"

Augusta Lawes turned bright pink, at which even brave Phoebe seemed to realize she had overstepped.

"I have been most eager for company," Hallie volunteered quickly. "I have been able to walk out for only the briefest periods in all this rain."

"And what a shame that is," August Lawes agreed.

" 'Tis fine countryside. As fine as anywhere. Though I will always cherish a special fondness for my own native Yorkshire."

There followed a polite, unfocused discussion of the relative merits and delights of several counties, only interrupted when Hoskins opened the door and announced "the Viscount Langsford." When Richard Marksley strode through to them, Hallie rose as though compelled.

"Ladies," he said. It was all he said. But with the smile and look that followed, Hallie felt he had told her a great deal more.

"Oh, Richard!" Phoebe flew to stand close to him. "Was London dreadfully exciting?"

"At least in part, Miss Lawes," he told her with an indulgent quirk to his lips. "Mostly dreadful."

Phoebe made a protesting moue and would have questioned him further, but her mother had apparently noticed what Hallie had as well—that despite his smile Richard Marksley looked tired.

"Phoebe, we must not keep Lord Langsford. You forget he has been traveling." Augusta Lawes smiled as she rose from the sofa. "You have been most gracious, my dear. We wish you both the very best. My lord, Miss Ashton tells us you intend to wed shortly."

"Tomorrow, Mrs. Lawes," Richard told her, though his gaze shot to Hallie. "I have a special license with me."

Hallie drew a quick breath. Only Phoebe's disappointed "Oh!" recalled her to her situation.

"Well, my lord," Augusta Lawes's look was curious. "You are certainly forward. Your aunt must be . . . well, at least—"

"She is resigned, Mrs. Lawes, which is all that we would ask of her and perhaps all of which she is capable at the moment. She has not come down?"

"The countess has been indisposed," Hallie supplied, her own voice sounding strangely husky to her ears. Richard Marksley's gaze lingered on her face, as though he studied her anew. Had he been away only five days? It had seemed a lifetime.

He turned to Mrs. Lawes. "I cannot persuade you and your daughter to stay to tea? I assure you I am not at all fatigued."

"Oh please, Mama! We must!" Phoebe urged. "There is so much to hear of town!"

"You forget, dearest, that we are promised to the Begwitts for dinner. And Simon Begwitt asked particularly to see you. You would not wish to disappoint him."

Torn between a conquest and a prize, Phoebe could do little more than worry her lower lip.

"Perhaps the ladies might return when their engagements are less pressing," Hallie suggested.

"We would be delighted," Mrs. Lawes said with a grateful look. Indeed, Richard Marksley looked grateful as well.

"You must promise me, Richard," Phoebe insisted as they moved with him to the door. "Even if you will be an old married man."

"I shall only be a few days older, Miss Lawes," Hallie heard him say as he escorted them out into the hall. "Pray do not accelerate my decline."

Hallie vaguely heard the steps, the carriage, the farewells and closing doors. Then Richard Marksley had returned to her.

He took her hand and raised it to his lips, teasing her fingers with a kiss so light it was little more than a breath.

" 'Come live with me,' " he said softly, " 'and be my love—' "

Hallie abruptly pulled her hand from his and stepped to the hearth.

"Never say she quoted it to you again," she said, striving for a composure she did not feel.

The subsequent pause seemed long.

"Phoebe Lawes is silly and harmless." His voice was low and reassuring. "She should not trouble you."

Hallie turned to him in surprise. It was as though the man had decided to woo her in the few hours remaining at his disposal. How very ironic that would be—that he should have spent the past five days accommodating himself to the prospect of marriage, while she had believed him wishing for the opposite.

"Phoebe Lawes does not trouble me," Hallie said. "I merely find her rendering lacks . . . sensibility."

"And my rendering?" Somehow Richard Marksley had moved close to her again. "How do you find my rendering?"

"I find it . . . unsettling."

"I see." He frowned and turned from her. "We have been apart for some days now, Miss Hallie. No doubt your thoughts with regard to our situation have intruded as often upon your peace as have mine. Yet we seem to have arrived at differing conclusions." He ran one hand through his hair and moved to stare out at the slumbering garden.

"I have resolved to find some good in this. Certainly both of us will be surrendering a great deal. I, for example, feel I must reexamine my role as publisher of *The Tantalus*. As for yourself—well, you have not told me enough of yourself for me to gauge how much of meaning to you must be abandoned in the arrangement. But I can truthfully see no way to avoid our marriage." He turned to face her. "I propose that, if we set our minds to it, there may be something of value, if only a modicum of respect and companionship, to be gained from our association. It is only rational."

For some reason the explanation prompted Hallie to shiver, though she stood next to the fire.

"I am certain you must be right, my lord," she said softly. "But I would ask one favor of you." At his raised brow she added, "I would ask you to continue with the journal. To continue your work on *The Tantalus*."

His smile was quizzical. "Why would that be of such importance to you, Miss Hallie, that you would ask it as a favor of me?"

Hallie made a dismissive gesture with one hand, then clasped the mantel edge with the other. "Do you not understand? You are a craftsman. With a skill. You have dedicated so much to it. So many depend on you to continue. 'Twould be tantamount to criminal to cease. You would—you would regret it."

Richard Marksley's look was still puzzled, perhaps a little sad. "And you believe limiting that role would affect our union?" he asked. "Because you fear I would be unhappy?"

Hallie nodded.

"Then I must convince you that there will be compensations. Though not perhaps of a grandeur to suit your uncle, my resources are considerable. Perhaps we will spend more time in London. Even a Viscount is permitted to attend salons, readings and concerts." He smiled. "I am not beyond finding some contentment and enrichment in other quarters."

"But it is not what you choose," Hallie protested. " 'Tis not your passion."

"Do not be anxious for my good spirits, my dear. I am a reading man. I will continue to correspond, perhaps even to pen something myself now and then. But the investment of time to oversee *The Tantalus* is considerable. You would rarely have my company." A sudden, skeptical coldness crossed his features. "Or is that, after all, your desire?"

Hallie raised her chin. "You insult me, my lord. I am not so calculating. I was thinking of your subscribers, of your contributors, and most of all of you yourself. To relinquish so much, out of a sense of duty! If you do not already resent me, my lord, you would come to."

"That is a decision I must make," he said. Hallie felt he watched her with a strained intensity. "I am trying, with your aid, to move beyond the circumstances that force me to that decision."

"But you will not forget them."

"Time will ease them." He startled her by smiling. "Miss Ashton—forgive me . . . Hallie—I believe you upset yourself to no purpose. We will wed tomorrow morning. Would you attempt to delay the inevitable? What possible alternative have you?"

"I . . . have been thinking. Perhaps as a governess—"

His gaze was kind as he shook his head. "Our betrothal has been the *on dit* in London for more than a week, my dear. Were we to cry off, scandal would inevitably result. No respectable family would have you." He sighed. "I commend you for making the argument. I only wish that I could say it is persuasive. Unfortunately, whatever deductive powers I possess lead me so far and no further."

"There are people," Hallie said carefully, "who have chosen to ignore the conventions. It is done, my lord."

"But I must disappoint you. For I fear, in this realm at least, I am a conventional man. Others have chosen more radical paths; I choose mine. It is a question of living comfortably with oneself. Even were you to hare off to the Continent tomorrow, I would feel you were owed the Marksley name."

The point was conclusive. With a sinking sensation, Hallie asked softly, "But is your heart free, my lord?"

"Free? It has been free many years."

Hallie noted that he did not say it was *now* free.

"Forgive me," she pressed her palms together. "But a number of people have taken pains to inform me of a certain lady—Caroline Chalmers."

"The former Caroline Chalmers, the Dowager Marchioness of Wrethingwell-Drummond, was married three years. If she is now, unhappily, widowed, it changes nothing."

"But you care for her?"

Marksley shrugged impatiently and moved toward her.

"I care for her only in a reflective way." He frowned. "Only as one cares for a memory."

"One saves it," Hallie said softly, "though its bloom is spent."

His riveted attention instantly alerted her to her error. It seemed too long a period before he asked, "What did you say?"

"I don't . . . recall. Do you mean about memory?"

"Yes. You quoted a poem—a line from a poem." His gaze was sharp. "Do you remember where you read it?"

"I fear I cannot. It must have been in *The Tantalus.*"

"I think I can be trusted to recognize what I myself publish."

Hallie forced a laugh. "Surely not every line, my lord."

He looked irritated, whether by the honorific or by her doubt she could not have said. "Perhaps you read it in another publication?"

"I believe I must have," she said with forced brightness.

"But you do not remember which it might have been?"

"Really, my lord, this—"

"Do not call me that. We are alone. I do not require it, nor do I like it, particularly from you."

"Why particularly?"

"Because you, more than anyone, know what it means to me." He turned from her to face the windows once more. "The line you quoted is one I last saw in some private correspondence. I had not known he intended to publish it elsewhere—or had, perhaps, already published it elsewhere." His manner was abstracted as he observed the cold rain.

"Of whom do you speak?" Hallie ventured.

Marksley glanced back at her.

"Of Beecham. Henry Beecham. We have discussed his work."

"Yes." Hallie wanted him to say more. She wanted his confidences, though she should not have wanted them—cutting reminders of her duplicity! In that instant she decided, in her own selfish interest, that though she might burden him with an unwanted wife, she need not deprive him of a poet.

"Ah. Here is your uncle," Marksley remarked without enthusiasm. Hallie heard her uncle's voice in the hall. As he entered the drawing room, she had the distinct sense of having her solitude invaded though Richard Marksley had been with her for some time.

"Well, my lord, so you have chosen to return." Alfred Ashton's words were not unfriendly, but he still sounded grudging. Hallie wondered what possible complaint he could have, as he had been an Earl's guest—with the attendant generous benefits—for almost a fortnight.

"Yes, Mr. Ashton, I have returned, and with a special license. Your niece and I will wed tomorrow morning. With your permission." Marksley bowed. "I spoke to Vicar Mayhew on my way through town."

"But . . . the settlements?"

"I saw your solicitor in London. I believe you will be satisfied." Marksley pulled a thick sheet of vellum from his coat and handed it to Ashton. "All of your requests have been followed to the letter." Hallie knew her uncle would be deaf to the chill in Marksley's voice.

"Well, then." Alfred Ashton seemed at a loss. "Tomorrow morning, you say? Harriet's dress ain't finished yet, so I hear. All these gewgaws and furbelows the women set such store by, as you know, my lord—"

Marksley's glance flashed to her. "I regret that. But I fear you must agree there is a certain premium on time."

"That may be. That may be. Don't want any hugger-mugger business, though. Rushing the event now does seem a mite slapdash."

"Does it, sir? Two weeks ago it could not have been soon enough. The 'event' as you term it, will not grow grander, I guarantee it."

"A few days more—"

"Cannot be arranged, sir."

The brisk response sent the blood to Ashton's face.

"Now see here, Marksley . . . Viscount . . . my lord. You had best not forget what's been done to the girl—"

"I am unremittingly conscious of it, sir," Marksley interrupted, "which is why we wed tomorrow."

"She'll do naught unless I say so!"

"Oh yes, she will, Ashton. Your niece no longer need obey you. From this day forward she no longer owes you anything she does not care to give. I intend to make that absolutely certain, sir. Good day to you." And with that pointed defense of his affianced, to whom he did not even grant a glance, the Viscount Langsford left the room.

Chapter Eight

The wedding was a trial.

The Countess, swathed in black bombazine, silently observed the dismal proceedings like a harbinger of doom. The few antique relatives carted in to lend countenance to the ceremony appeared likely to follow Reginald shortly to the grave. Vicar Mayhew sounded hoarse, an ailment no doubt exacerbated by an early blast of wintry weather, weather that left the church dark and drafty. Hallie's sapphire silk gown, the finest she owned, clung damply to her ankles after the walk from the carriage in the rain.

One of the horses had gone lame.

Miss Binkin had the effrontery to cry.

Richard Marksley looked as though he had not slept. By the time he slipped the ring on her finger and granted the faintest, perfunctory kiss to her chilled lips, Hallie felt mortified. She signed the register as though in a trance and fled the gloomy little church to the relative light of a drizzly morning. She clasped her drowned nosegay as though it were a friend. The morning's single smile came from a young girl walking along the vicarage lane.

Breakfast at Penham consisted of a bountiful buffet that could not tempt Hallie in the slightest, and, by the time their few guests had departed, she had been ready to take to her bed with a very real, painful megrim. But Richard Marksley had no intention of remaining another minute under the same roof with his sullen aunt and Hallie's overbearing uncle. He had whisked her away to his home at Archers.

Recalling all of it now, Hallie shifted her shoulders against the tree trunk and basked in the warm sunlight on her arms and face. Today's return of good weather had brightened her mood considerably, as had a good night's dreamless sleep. She had not seen Richard Marksley after their flight from Penham the previous day. She had excused herself to nurse her headache only to find that she slept through supper. Marksley had gone out, just where she did not inquire, and this morning he had left for a ride when she came down to breakfast. Hallie wondered whether this would be the pattern of their days—determining just how little time they need spend in each other's presence.

Yet he was working on *The Tantalus.* Hallie knew that, and indulged her curiosity. He had said he would be unable to continue, yet he seemed to be addressing the last days of the journal with energy.

At some point in the future, he would be pressed to leave Archers and remove permanently to Penham. But in this interlude, however brief, Hallie could enjoy the manor's quiet charms and the lovely old orchard where she had secluded herself.

The relief she felt now, after weeks of strain, was substantial. That morning she had written out carefully, in Henry Beecham's larger and less legible hand, the poem she had begun at Penham. The sentiment had been true for days. Her thoughts on the matter at last had shaped themselves so clearly that mere words flowed easily. With this poem, she thought, Richard Marksley would know that Beecham had not betrayed him; Beecham had never left him. No one could express such confidence and joy in one person yet seek out another.

She had folded the single sheet and sealed it with a wafer, addressing it to R.E. Marksley, Archers, Surrey. Hallie planned to ask Jeremy to post it once he returned to town. Beecham's bond with Marksley had not yet suffered. Some still hopeful part of her dreamed that Marksley need never know how close he was to his reclusive poet. Then she might continue writing poems—and writing poems to him.

She fingered the letter between the pages of her journal. She had brought her writing box outside with her, but the sunlight and comfortable temperature, the serenity and low chirping of sparrows, were all so heavenly she had scarcely written a word. She untied the ribbons of her bonnet, slid it from her hair and raised her face to the sun. Her shoulders relaxed. She would bake all worry and distress into something deliciously sweet... honeycake or—

"My lady," she heard Gibbs say tentatively, "Ahem . . . my lady."

She opened her eyes to find the elderly butler standing respectfully to the side.

"Yes, Gibbs?"

"You have a letter from the post, my lady. Forwarded from Penham. I thought you might wish to see it right away."

"Thank you, Gibbs. You are very thoughtful." She took the letter without rising and watched Gibbs depart before breaking the seal. She had recognized Jeremy's hand.

Dearest Hallie,

I start myself tomorrow, but wanted you to know as soon as possible that I have found your partridge. Together we have seen to the little matter that concerned you. Do not expect a small fortune, but I assure you it will suffice.

George proposes to accompany me as far as Denhurst, where a gypsy band long familiar to him is now encamped. Expect me then, with the bounty, on Saturday.

Yours,
Jeremy

P.S. I enclose one of Richard's letters held at the General Post Office in London. Though you now need never tell him a thing, I urge you to do so. Surely you owe him that? I do not care to remember you as craven, Hallie.

The note trembled in her hand. Jeremy had every right to admonish her. He was right to give his sympathies to Richard Marksley, who deserved so much of what she did not: respect and friendship.

But now she had to think. Today was Saturday. Jeremy might arrive at any moment. And he would be shocked at just how craven she had proved to be.

The new gold band on her finger felt strangely weighty. Thought of a precious, perfect Caroline Chalmers rose unbidden. 'She walks in beauty like the night . . .' Ah! Why had Archie Cavendish cursed her with Byron's idolizing imagery?

Marksley was unlikely to have forgotten such a paragon. Yet here he was, bound by laws of church and crown to a most imperfect substitute.

Her gaze fell to the letter Jeremy had enclosed. It had been posted in London. The familiar and unexpectedly dear hand clearly spelled out 'Henry Beecham.' She wondered again what devilish ambition or yearning had possessed her to perpetrate this fraud. With trembling fingers she broke open the seal:

Dear Beecham,

It is difficult to encourage another when one is discouraged, but that is the task before me. My low spirits result from the necessity to limit my rela-

tionship with The Tantalus, *perhaps even to discontinue its publication altogether. Thus the circumstances entail some disruption for you. The journal may yet live, but at this point I dare not pledge. As I have described to you in the past, the labor has largely been one of love—a burden not easily surrendered, however eagerly assumed.*

I will attempt to relay any news. For now, publication will be suspended after the next number. Should you have any difficulty placing work elsewhere, be assured I shall not leave you stranded. I have only ever encountered enthusiasm on your behalf.

As always, I urge you to continue along those lines that most appeal to you. With ability as promising as yours, I am reluctant to direct it in any manner. The sole encouragement your talent needs is to be permitted to grow.

Beecham, I have told you how greatly I admire your artistry. I am too practical a man to spend much time on regrets—the future will demand enough concentration—but I do know that I regret never having met you. Should you ever find occasion to redress that lack I would be most honored.

As ever yours & c.
R.E. Marksley

He had signed it without reference to his title. Hallie reread the letter several times, searching, ironically, for some evidence of those new responsibilities of which she was so much a part. But the tone of it was no different from any other letter Beecham had ever received. That she now found it frustratingly remote and unrevealing was less a measure of any alteration in Richard Marksley than in herself. He had, after all, no reason to suspect that in writing to Beecham, he was now writing to his wife.

She carefully placed the letters inside her journal, tucked against her new poem, and leaned back once more against the old apple's generous bole. It was, she thought, suitably an apple tree, for she was tempted to absolve herself of responsibility. After all, the roguish Reginald Marksley had brought her to this impasse. She should instead be blessing her good fortune: in ridding herself of her uncle and Millicent, in ascending to position and privilege, in marrying the man she loved. But even as she admitted as much she knew there was something drastically wrong.

She was frowning when a shadow blocked the sun.

"You look like a dryad," he told her and watched her eyes open. "Siphoning sunlight instead of moonlight, playing truant rather than tending to your tree."

"You are being fanciful," she murmured, sitting up. She brushed her skirts and looked about her. When her gaze fell upon a thick notebook, Richard noticed it as well.

"I wonder," he said, leaning to pick it up, "what you record in your journal?"

"Words," she said quickly and held up her hands to receive the book from him, "just words."

He had an intense desire to open the book, to read her hand and perhaps a bit of her heart. The desire was so strong that he had to force himself to release the volume to her eager fingers. He was reminded of another, equally strong and troubling desire, one that had persisted from the time he had kissed her so chastely in the church. He had been ceaselessly drawn by the thought of kissing her again.

His spouse seemed overly relieved to have her journal in hand. The fact engaged his curiosity. Perhaps she kept mementos of some sort inside. Then he scowled as he wondered if any were of Reggie.

"I suppose you saw many of your acquaintance in London last week?" she asked him.

"I did," he responded, surprised by the question. "Naturally, with the impending changes at *The Tantalus* and the alteration in my circumstances there was much to which to attend."

She seemed uncertain, even troubled as she played with a blade of grass and looked away from him. "And did you inform them of our marriage?"

"I did," he repeated, puzzled by the direction of her questions. "Those few whom I wished to inform. As I mentioned, our alliance was cause for some sensational attention amongst the *ton*. We are better out of it." He examined her face. "There is no need for you to prepare correspondence, if that is what concerns you."

"Did you tell Caroline Chalmers?"

At once he understood. But he did not answer as quickly. Instead he moved to sit down on the ground beside her, and attempted to find a comfortable position for his long legs and booted feet.

"There is no Caroline Chalmers," he told her again, resting his arms on his raised knees. "Only Lady Wrethingwell-Drummond, the Dowager Marchioness of Wrethingwell-Drummond. And pray," he smiled at her, "do not force me to say that mouthful too often."

"You told me that you had cared . . . I mean, the accepted thinking seemed to be—"

"The accepted thinking is nonsense. I am not in love with the woman, although many years ago I inanely believed myself to be. She was, in fact, almost the death of me. Had I been even an ounce more reckless, my days might have been considerably shorter." As her eyes widened, he explained, "Miss Caroline enjoyed the affections of many. Her preference seemingly settled on me, to my great joy, until one of my thick-witted rivals took it into his head to demand a duel. When I realized that Caroline thrilled at the prospect that one or both of us might die for her, my attachment suffered a sea change. I purchased my commission that day and left for the Peninsula even before my affairs were settled. Caroline spurned the bloodthirsty fool, who, by the way, now has a wife and two children. He lives in Richmond, my dear," he added, looking directly at her, "you might have occasion to meet him. Not a scar on 'im, whereas I have several. Anyway," he looked away as his wife's cheeks turned pink, "Caroline wrote that she would wait for me, though we were never pledged. But within three months she had wed old Bellis, a man with little to recommend him, apart from an ancient title and a fat purse."

"You were not bitter?"

"Oh certainly. I was young, besotted with a woman whom independent observers termed one of the most beautiful in the land. But Caroline had always been too free with everything fortune bestowed on her—feeling, friendship, favors—and managed to devalue them all. I consider myself well away from her. My only regret is that my name continues to be bandied about with hers. Even in places like Squire Lawes's dining room," he added pointedly, "though she has been widowed mere months."

"And now you have been compelled to this."

"I have compelled myself. It was and is the right thing to do." He looked at her very steadily. "You may hear the lady's name again. I hope that will not distress you. You are now my wife, which fact should silence any further speculation. You may be spared what I was not."

He read more in her gaze, but whatever the thought, she did not voice it. Perhaps she did not believe she could trust him to preserve her from speculation of a different nature.

"Hallie," he said. "We have not discussed one aspect of this arrangement that may concern you. A wife's obligations—"

"My lord," she interrupted quickly, "Miss Binkin has explained."

"*Miss* Binkin has?" How astonishing, then, that his

wife was not pale and trembling. "The formidable Miss Binkin has unanticipated talents," he said mildly. "But let me assure you that I have no intention of claiming anything you have no wish to give. And that until you are ready, if ever you so choose, I will conduct myself discreetly."

She looked away from him and continued to play with the grass. "Thank you, my lord." Her reserve bothered him.

"Please call me Richard. 'Twould please me."

"Thank you . . . Richard."

His name still sounded like "my lord." He was pondering, still disturbed, why she should discomfit him so, when she surprised him by saying, "Mrs. Lawes tells me there is a gypsy encampment just beyond Denhurst. Should it not be a great trouble to you . . . Richard . . . I would very much enjoy a visit to see it."

"Gypsies?" he asked. "They interest you?"

"Yes." She tilted her chin as though he had challenged her. "They live so differently. And a friend of mine, and of my late father's, has studied them. But I have never seen them."

"Then we shall most definitely visit. That may be a couple of days from now, however, as I have some business to see to."

"Thank you." She again looked away.

"Hallie," he said, then paused. Something in him chose to savor the name. "Hallie, if possible I should like to share my home with more than a polite stranger. Is it possible we might make an effort?"

She nodded her head, but still refused to look at him, and he, who had had evidence of her confidence, of her spirit, recognized his disappointment in her reticence. What was wrong with her today? The wedding had changed her. The ordeal had been brutish.

His lips thinned as he rose to leave her. He thought time alone might restore her balance, but he stood still when she stared up at him. Her eyes were suspiciously bright as she clutched her book to her bodice.

"What is it, my dear?" he asked softly.

"You know little about me, my lord—Richard."

"I hope to know you better," he said easily, though her expression made him feel anything but easy.

"And you must truly surrender *The Tantalus?*"

"It is likely." He frowned as she lowered her head. "But you mustn't fret over this. The time I spent with it is not something you would have understood." He watched with concern as she averted her face. "I should leave you to collect yourself. Please do not worry about this matter. I have told you before, you should not permit it to distress you."

He bowed, though she did not turn to him, and left her still sitting there. In doing so, he wondered if he were not failing his new bride, but her anxiety regarding *The Tantalus* struck him as disproportionate to her interests. He was, after all, trying to make some time to entertain a wife. She would simply have to calm herself.

"Milord," Gibbs greeted him at the back terrace

doors. "Lord Jeremy has arrived. With luggage." He sniffed dramatically.

Richard ran a hand through his already tousled hair. "This is most unexpected, Gibbs. He sent no word."

"There was a letter to Lady Langsford, milord. To the Viscountess."

"To Lady—" For a moment Richard stared at him. "Indeed. Well, Gibbs, we owe you an apology. I am certain my lady would never have intentionally failed to inform you."

"No, milord. Certainly not. The letter just arrived, milord. Addressed to Miss Ashton." Again Richard stared at him.

"Where is he then, Gibbs?" he managed at last.

"He awaits you in the parlor, milord."

Richard walked on into the house. Something was amiss: that he should find his wife eager to visit gypsies, see her near tears over his abandonment of *The Tantalus*, then have Jeremy descend upon them—a visit she had failed to relay to him. Yes, something was clearly amiss, but he was dashed if he knew what it was.

Jeremy Asquith, strikingly attired in rose jacquard waistcoat, cream cravat, bottlegreen coat and gold buckskins, stood resplendently considering the portrait of Richard's mother.

"What a charming creature she must have been," he observed as Richard stopped in the doorway. Jeremy glanced over his shoulder at him. "I have never seen any resemblance."

"More's the pity," Richard said, stepping warily into the room. He felt as though everyone and everything around him were part of an elaborate trap. "I am the spitting image of my father."

Jeremy surveyed the matching portrait opposite. "That is not much of a hardship, my friend. I have told you so before. You should contemplate your good fortune daily."

"I would happily contemplate it, Jeremy, if I had a spare minute in which to contemplate much of anything. But the past few weeks have been devilishly busy." As he spoke, he subjected Jeremy to a cynical gaze. "My good fortune at present consists of ascending to a title I never chose, relinquishing the avocation I did choose, and landing myself a wife who would never have chosen *me*."

Jeremy stared at him.

"You married her," he said flatly.

"Miss Ashton is now the Viscountess Langsford," Richard affirmed, wondering why it should bother him that Jeremy looked suddenly too pale. "When Reginald died I had no choice."

"I . . . see." Jeremy cleared his throat. "And when were you married?"

"Yesterday. Had you been here, I would have asked you to stand up with me."

"I would have been honored, Richard. And you have my sincere congratulations. Hallie Ashton is a most unusual prize, as you may perhaps have discovered?"

It seemed to Richard that Jeremy's query, accompanied as it was by a look of curious anticipation, was too suggestive. "Just what would you be intimating, Asquith?" he asked sharply, then immediately checked himself.

One of Jeremy's russet eyebrows shot high.

"Easy, my friend. I spoke only in generalities. Far be it from me to intrude upon your privacy."

"Deuce take it, Jeremy! You know why I married the girl. Must you make a joke of this?"

"I am not making a joke of it. Although it seems that you, foolishly, are determined to do so." With his distinctive gait, Jeremy moved to a wing chair and, displaying some ceremony, took a seat. "I think I shall remove to the Threepenny Arms in town. I have no wish to spoil the honeymoon."

Richard glowered at him, but Jeremy merely twirled a quizzing glass from long, graceful fingers.

"Quit with that, Jeremy," Richard said impatiently. "You know your vision is superb."

Jeremy smiled, but put the glass away. "I should like to know three things, Richard. First, the particulars regarding Reginald's demise. Second, your obviously-flawed reasoning behind the absurdity of abandoning *The Tantalus*. And third . . . how is your wife?"

"My wife is fine," Richard snapped.

"I should like to see for myself before my departure. With your permission, of course, Richard. But the other matters?"

Richard told him curtly of Reginald's mishap. He expanded a bit more upon his decision to withdraw from *The Tantalus*. When the tea tray arrived with victuals enough for twelve, Jeremy continued his protests between bites of food.

"It will not do, Richard," he argued. "There is no need for such an extreme. You would not be the first peer to engage in literary endeavors. Indeed, the pursuit is enjoying a certain fashion, as you well know. There must be something more, *compadre mio*. You are not being entirely frank."

Richard shrugged his shoulders. "I do not have the heart to continue, Jeremy. To battle so much at once. You might wish to know, since you claimed to enjoy the fellow's work as well, that Beecham has published elsewhere. I discovered it quite by chance. If *he* cannot be loyal to *The Tantalus*, or at least have clarified his outsized aspirations, I haven't the desire to continue. I shan't nurture ungrateful whelps."

Jeremy choked on a piece of biscuit. A fit of coughing resulted, only eased after some minutes and several large gulps of tea. By that time Richard had at last taken a seat.

"Are you absolutely certain," Jeremy's voice sounded hoarse, "that Beecham bolted? To whom?"

"I do not yet know, although I have taken steps to determine that. Miss Ashton—Lady Langsford—quoted something to me that Beecham had sent me in a letter. She could not recall the source. Unless Beecham has appropriated someone else's work—which I cannot bring myself to believe, given the quality of his correspondence—he must have published elsewhere."

"I . . . see." Jeremy was grimacing, an expression of such concentrated discomfort that he looked truly hideous.

"You look most peculiar, Jeremy. Is there something you wish to say?"

"I?"

Richard looked away from him, out to the garden, and drummed the fingers of his right hand against the chair arm.

"My wife thinks me a complete cad," he mused aloud, unconsciously changing the subject.

"Hallie was always a most observant young lady."

Richard shot Jeremy a look of exasperation. "I have not been anything less than reasonable," he protested.

"Surely not. How could you be? The renowned R.E. Marksley, now heir to Penham, deigning to marry so lowly a creature in order to preserve her good name. Why, she must be overjoyed."

"You are quite wrong," Richard bit out. "If we had not wed, Miss Ashton would have been sold off to some farmer's son or sent to a nunnery."

"Are you so certain?"

"I had as much from her uncle."

"And you have made it quite clear to her just how much of a favor you have bestowed?"

"Not in the manner you infer. But she must know that to be the case. And it has not been so very awful for her.

I have been most solicitous." He did not volunteer that he had just left his wife weeping. He rose and moved to look out at the lawns.

"Richard, my friend, any woman—every woman—no matter her station in life, desires to be honored, to be thought worthy of respect and affection."

"Undoubtedly," Richard said, then looked more closely at Jeremy. "You suspect me of failing in that regard?"

"It certainly sounds it."

"I assure you I have been most *scrupulously* respectful of my wife." Richard firmed his lips and again focused on the view out back. He could see that Hallie had roused herself and was walking slowly back along a hedgerow and path that led to the house.

He heard Jeremy once again choking on something.

"For heaven's sake, Jeremy, if you cannot eat properly, at least try to consume less."

"I was simply surprised, Richard. How long do you anticipate this state of . . . suspension will continue?"

"As long as the lady desires it." He continued to watch her approach the house. She stopped every few feet to look at the sky, or survey a view, or watch a bird or squirrel. He found himself wanting to know what she was thinking.

"Richard," Jeremy drew his attention again. "I have been mulling over Beecham. It simply does not make any sense to me that he would send work elsewhere. You and *The Tantalus* have been too good to him."

"I should say," Richard agreed.

"So might it not be simple happenstance that the wording of a phrase is similar?"

"Possibly," Richard said idly, his attention now inexplicably absorbed by his wife's slow progress.

"Richard," Jeremy said, this time more urgently, "have you ever wondered whether Henry Beecham might be a woman?"

Watching Hallie stoop just then to pick up and examine a fallen leaf, Richard did not at first register the question. The words seemed to echo about in his head for a moment before he comprehended their meaning. He studied his new wife and wondered what sort of a woman would pretend to be a man.

"Impossible," he said shortly.

"Why less possible than that two different people should pen the same words?"

Richard turned to stare at Jeremy.

"I have never considered it," he said. "Why should you do so? What would be the motive in dissembling?"

"Is not publication enough of a motive for a writer such as Beecham?"

"*The Tantalus* would have published Beecham whatever his—or her—sex."

"Truly, Richard? I always believed as much. Then perhaps if a woman felt herself to be flouting her family's, or even society's, rules and expectations? A serious pursuit of literature is rarely encouraged in a female."

"True," Richard said. "But have you ever had any indication that Beecham might be other than a man? I had no notion you maintained a correspondence."

"I have never corresponded with Henry Beecham. I know, from you, that he is hermitical in the extreme. It simply occurred to me that such an explanation might account for your difficulty in locating the chap."

Richard smiled grimly. "If anyone, man or woman, chooses not to be found, it can be remarkably difficult to defeat that purpose. I have tried."

"Perhaps we might ask your wife's opinion, as I understand she has . . . a fondness for poetry."

"An excellent idea. You might ask her yourself, as she is just returned, and I, unfortunately, have some letters to write." He moved even as he spoke, reaching the doorway as Hallie entered. He noticed her eager expression and dry eyes as her gaze sought Jeremy. Richard had no desire to observe their fond reunion.

"My dear," he said, "here is our good friend wishing to satisfy himself of your welfare. I pray you will set his mind at ease. But please excuse me from your company. Some pressing matters will not wait." He bowed, but not before he noted the sudden shadows in her beautiful eyes, whether from distress or anger he did not know and did not stay to discover.

Jeremy unfurled his long length from his chair and stood to survey her through a quizzing glass. For some endless period he did not say a word, even after she had moved to stand before him.

"Well," he said at last. "I thought at first you were someone known to me. But now I see that you are clearly a stranger."

"Do not scold, Jeremy," Hallie implored him. She pressed her palms together and started to pace. "I could conceive of no way to avoid this. In my place what would you have done?"

"I would not have been in your place, Hallie. I believe I gave you the benefit of my sage advice some time ago."

If anything she paced with more agitation. "Yes, you are quite right. I have been unutterably foolish. But now?"

"Now, m'dear," he drawled, "I wish you happy."

"Happy? Jeremy, I am afraid that is most improbable."

"You cannot love him?"

Hallie knew she was blushing, but had no control over her color. Instead she collapsed upon the nearest sofa and gazed beseechingly at him.

"Perhaps," Jeremy said slowly, "I should rephrase. *Do* you love him?"

Hallie's fingers tensed against the upholstered cushions.

"God help me," she whispered.

Jeremy ceased playing with his quizzing glass and smiled at her. "I shall take that as an affirmative," he remarked dryly. "And I am encouraged. You might trust your heart in this, Hallie. And Richard. He is an excellent man." As he noted her anxiety, his smile faded. "I fail to understand the obstacle," he said, sounding for the moment every inch a duke's son.

"There is a major obstacle. In Henry Beecham."

Jeremy reached to toss some crumb of food into his mouth before responding. "'Tis true that Richard seems distraught about that ingrate's behavior. He would have it that Beecham's duplicity in sending work elsewhere has contributed to the decision to forsake *The Tantalus*. A very unfortunate slip, my dear. You shall have to set things to rights."

"Yes, I know. Only . . . was he very angry?"

"Angry? I shouldn't say so. Rather intensely disappointed, disheartened, tricked, betrayed, deceived, duped, gulled, hoodwinked—"

"Thank you, Jeremy," Hallie said quickly. "I understand you. I just must think what is best to do next."

"Do not puzzle too long, Hallie. As a concerned observer, I must tell you that your maneuverings to date have proved disastrous." He pulled a wad of bank notes from his waistcoat pocket and handed the funds to her. "There is enough there for passage most anywhere worth going, if you should so choose. I had Partridge ask for tenners, to avoid arousing suspicion. Women rarely carry so much blunt, as you know only too well. You may wish to count it."

"You are too cruel, Jeremy." She swallowed. "You know how grateful I am."

"I suppose I should apologize for dawdling about it," he said blandly.

"That would be preposterous. You must know I never intended to take so much of your time, to send you scouring half the country. I can never repay you and I . . . I am ashamed." She looked down at her lap. "How is George?"

"Settled in nicely with his Romanies. This group is

only five miles or so away from you, the other side of the Downs. He was most amenable to posing as Beecham, never asked me for an explanation beyond your need of the funds. A most obliging fellow. I might hope that some fair day you will trouble to thank him."

"You know I shall, Jeremy. You have both been very good to me."

He considered her for a moment.

"I must go now, Hallie. I am retreating to the Threepenny Arms. I cannot bear to watch my two good friends engage in such insupportable farce."

"I understand. One way or another I promise I shall make amends. As part of that," she reached for her journal, "would you kindly post this when you return to London." She pulled the sealed poem from the pages. "Only . . . only with your regular letters," she added, aware of imposing on him again. " 'Twould perhaps reassure him that Beecham never left him—that is, never left *The Tantalus*."

Jeremy took the missive and read its direction. He tapped it against one palm.

" 'Tis just another poem," Hallie explained.

"I see." He continued to tap the envelope, then said coldly, "Hallie this must stop."

"It will stop. But it must be satisfactory. I would rather he kept *The Tantalus* than that I should keep . . . that I should—Oh, Jeremy! I thought to keep Beecham, but I grasped at more. And now, I have lost myself."

"You have lost nothing, Hallie, except your heart. It is not such an unusual item to lose."

"Except . . . you must tell me. Did he love Caroline Chalmers very much?"

Jeremy studied her.

"I should imagine not," he said casually, slipping the poem into his waistcoat pocket. "I have observed Richard in love."

Hallie absorbed that in silence.

"Well then," she managed, "I had thought to stay and perhaps retain a friendship. But if he should never forgive—"

Jeremy took her hand and lightly squeezed her fingers.

"You should be kinder to yourself, my dear," he suggested softly. "You are his wife. Richard is unlikely to realize there is anything to forgive." With a last, warm press of her hand he departed.

Chapter Nine

Hallie held the bank notes close to her skirts and fled upstairs to her room. She placed her journal at her bedside, then went directly to the writing desk and pushed the money to the back of a drawer. When she moved to the washstand, her face in the glass looked rosy and excited.

You are his wife, Jeremy had said. Was he correct to believe she was unkind to herself? Perhaps the years with her uncle and Millicent had trained her too thoroughly, that she should now believe she deserved so little.

She could not find the prospect so undesirable after all—to be mistress at Archers. To be countess at *Penham*. But there she suffered a qualm. For though she had discovered how dearly she wanted the first, she was not at all certain she wanted the last. There was much more to this than being a wife. . . .

She took her time changing for supper, dispensing with an offer of help from one of the maids. When the first bell sounded, she went down, making an effort at composure, yet as she neared the dining room, Richard Marksley stepped from the library. They halted, glances locking, and Hallie knew she could not move unless he willed it. She at last breathed easily when he walked toward her.

"You shall put me to the blush, my dear, with your punctuality. The lady of the house must always take whatever time she requires—not that you would need it." He inclined his head, acknowledging that she must not have looked as anxious as she felt.

"I . . . find myself quite famished," she said, preceding him quickly into the dining room.

"And no wonder," he countered as Thomas held the chair for her. Her place was set to Marksley's left. "You missed dinner, if Mrs. Hepple's information is accurate. You must realize that the household is most anxious to please their lady. How is it possible for them to impress you if you do not eat or place any demands upon them?" He smiled.

"I am not used to being waited upon, my lord. My uncle's household in Tewsbury consists of three: chef, housemaid, and one manservant. I did not have an abigail, nor were there other personal servants."

"I cannot believe you intimidated by the prospect of commanding even so much as an army, my dear.

But you have not attempted to explain a lack of appetite."

"I . . . cannot explain it."

For a moment he merely looked at her, his dark eyes thoughtful. Then he turned his attention to the first course. Hallie followed his example and took a few bites of fish.

"I have not tried this before—" he said, smiling almost shyly. "That is, I have not tried marriage before, so I hope you will forgive me in advance for the many failings I doubtless will exhibit, at least within these first few weeks. After that . . . well, perhaps you must devise penalties."

"You are not the only one new to marriage, my lord. It is not something one practices."

"No. Though I gather that women are, from an early age, trained in some of the finer arts that ease its workings, whereas men are not."

"Every couple must be unique, my lord," she offered softly. "I understand a certain mutual respect is a place to start."

"Then may I request—again—that you respect my wish that you call me Richard?"

"Yes, of course, my . . . Richard." Something about his regard made her uneasy. As she turned her attention once more to the meal, she questioned whether their acquaintance might not have been rather special had it not been rooted in deceit.

" 'Tis a shame," he said, "that Lord Jeremy could not stay longer. I believe he felt himself an intruder."

"I have only ever known him to be an infrequent and temporary visitor," Hallie said. "Much like his capricious favorites, the butterflies."

"Capricious," Marksley repeated, fastening on the word. "Yet he is your fondest admirer."

"Is he?"

Marksley smiled and bowed his head to her.

"My lady correctly notes that on this our honeymoon, *I* am her fondest admirer. Let me say then that Jeremy is a loyal and fervent admirer."

"You exaggerate, my lord."

"If you so easily doubt my judgment, I dare not tell you how lovely you look tonight, Hallie."

Again an unwelcome warmth stole into her cheeks. "You need not . . ."

"No," he agreed shortly. "I know I need not. I say that to you because it is true, and because it gives me pleasure. I have no desire to spend our days denying either truth or my own pleasure. 'Twould be abhorrent." He looked determined.

The footman, oblivious to any tension at the table, quickly removed their dishes and started to serve the soup. When Gibbs unexpectedly entered the room, Marksley motioned him to the side of the table.

"Pardon me, my lord. I have news of Mr. Beecham," the butler said.

The spoon with which Hallie had been playing slipped from her grasp, striking the edge of a plate with a clatter.

"Of what nature?" Marksley asked.

"A runner from your bank in London has just delivered this, my lord." He handed a small card to Marksley, who quickly scanned its message.

"My letters of credit to Beecham were presented and honored two days ago in the City, to their full amount," Marksley explained as he read. For a moment he fell silent. Then he said wearily, "Thank you, Gibbs."

Hallie surreptitiously studied her husband's face as she sipped broth. Jeremy had relayed Marksley's sense of betrayal, his belief in the poet's desertion, and that description seemed too painfully accurate. Marksley had to be interpreting Beecham's exchange as a termination. But his thoughts were apparently far from the subject of Henry Beecham.

"You shall not lack for employment, Hallie, should you choose it. This community could use your wisdom and imagination in whatever capacity you, as Viscountess Langsford, might find congenial. I fear my aunt and uncle have been remiss with regard to certain responsibilities of station, particularly here in the country. I should like to do better."

Hallie essayed a smile.

"And you shall find no dearth of companionship or entertainment. Mrs. Lawes and Mrs. Mayhew will be most anxious to introduce you to a wide circle of acquaintances. The stable and garden here at Archers, indeed, the entire household at Penham as well, are at your disposal. Denhurst is a small but lively community. And the countryside is appealing." He mused a moment. "I think we must get you a horse."

Even as he listed all these potential pursuits, Hallie sensed his distraction.

"You sound fond of Denhurst . . . Richard."

He summoned a smile as he glanced at her. "I am. It is my home. I hope you will also come to care for it. But you need not resign yourself to the country. I must of necessity spend some portion of time in London. Perhaps we shall go up in February or March. There is a house at Berkeley Square, which you will, naturally, be free to adorn and rearrange as you choose."

"I am . . . overwhelmed." She did indeed feel overwhelmed, if not a little desperate. As he went on to describe the many lively attractions in London, the life Richard Marksley sketched sounded increasingly busy, comfortable—and empty. Just where did he intend to be as she "adorned" the town house and sampled the *ton's* offerings? She found she had little appetite for the minted lamb that comprised the main course. But conscious of her husband's gaze upon her, Hallie made an effort to eat.

"I have not asked if you play an instrument," Marksley said. "The piano in the parlor was my mother's. I would be pleased if you would consider it your own."

"I thank you. I fear I play only passably. But I shall be delighted to attempt improvement. Do you have any of your mother's music?"

"Some, I believe. I kept many of her things." He fingered his wineglass. "She was a talented and courageous woman, though never physically strong. My father would have been lost without her, as she was without him. I realized even as a child that their passing so closely together was a mercy for them."

"You miss them still."

"I do." Marksley looked up to meet her gaze. "Not the least for the selfish reason that I believe I should have been a better person for their company."

You are a fine person now, Hallie observed silently. For a moment she pushed the food about on her plate. Then she placed her serviette on the table and rose. "I am a bit chilled. I shall just return to my room for my shawl."

He looked astonished as he also rose. "'Tis simple enough to send Thomas or one of the maids for the shawl, my dear. You need not trouble yourself."

"The brief exercise will warm me," she insisted, even as she backed away from the table. "And as I mentioned, I am used to seeing to myself."

"This once, then, Hallie. And please come join me for coffee in the library when you are ready. There are some items I would like to show you."

Hallie nodded and fled into the hall.

She had been mad—*mad*—to think that she could go on like this, day after day, and keep her secret intact. She reached her room and found her unnecessary shawl. She had wanted only the break from polite constraint. Again she looked in the mirror and drew a deep breath. How to tell him—how to tell him? She could not decide. But it must be now.

As she reached the lower steps to the hall, Marksley was just exiting the dining room. He noted her flushed cheeks.

"There was no need to race, Hallie. At this rate, Gibbs might be tempted to back you at Epsom." She thought she heard a quickly shushed laugh from the dining room. "Would you now care for something more refreshing than coffee?"

Hallie met his smile with a tentative one of her own. "I still prefer coffee, thank you."

Marksley extended a hand to her as she descended the stairs. When his hand grasped hers the immediate warmth of the contact startled her. Before she could stumble, Marksley's arm clasped her waist.

"Careful," he said softly.

He practically lifted her from the last step. Hallie could scarcely breathe. She backed from him quickly and made a futile effort to arrange her shawl.

"Allow me." He took the garment from her suddenly clumsy hands and draped it across her shoulders, his fingers teasing the curls at her nape as he positioned the soft wool.

"I am surprised you have need of it, Hallie, as warm as you are." He must not have felt her shiver or he had known it was not due to cold. For an instant, his dark glance met hers. Holding his gaze, she thought it likely she would forget everything Miss Binkin had told her.

His palm at the small of her back urged her forward, else every piece of her would have turned to him again.

She led the way into the library, a room she had not entered since her initial meeting with him less than three weeks before. Yet it had been an age, she thought, and resolutely took a seat by the fire.

Marksley walked over to his desk. "I wanted you to see where we are located—at Archers, Penham, Denhurst—and to see where I believe your gypsy band is camped." He pulled some documents from a drawer as he spoke and now stood with them in one hand. "Then, since you know horses, I thought you might also like a look at the plans for Penham's new paddocks—"

Gibbs had knocked on the open door and entered the room with the coffee tray. Beecham's letter to Marksley was propped against the silver service.

Jeremy! Hallie raged, instantly, silently. She sat forward in her chair.

"What the devil—?" Marksley muttered. He placed his documents slowly upon the desk and reached for the folded note. He handled it carefully for a second, as though it were a live thing that might suddenly take flight.

"Gibbs."

"Yes, my lord."

"This letter—did it arrive with the runner from the bank, from London?"

Gibbs, pouring out the coffee, glanced at the document as though it had committed some unforgivable trespass.

"No, my lord. 'Twas left in the drawing room, on the mantel. No one reported its arrival. I know you are most particular about such matters."

"Yes, Gibbs. Indeed. But how did it get here? 'Twas not posted. No one has been in the drawing room today, surely?"

"A maid would have pulled the drapes, my lord, and just now Thomas entered to prepare for the coffee, before I directed him to the library."

"Send both of them in to me, if you would please, Gibbs."

When the butler departed Marksley turned to test the latches on the French doors to the garden. Then he faced Hallie, his manner distracted.

"I beg your pardon, my dear. An unexpected matter . . . Your coffee . . ."

"I have no need of it." Hallie moved to rise. "Richard—"

"No, do not leave me, Hallie. I shall join you in just a minute. Ah, Thomas, Mary." Thomas bowed as Mary curtsied. "Did either of you notice whether the drawing room doors were open to the garden earlier?"

"No, milord," they chimed. "They was locked," Mary added.

"Nor whether this letter was on the mantel when you were in earlier today?"

"I didna see it when I was pullin' at the drapes," Mary said, "Mighta been—"

"Only caught my eye on the mantel just now, milord.

Can't say as I would notice one more paper in the usual way," Thomas offered candidly.

"Just so," Marksley observed, with a rueful glance at his paper-strewn desk. "Did either of you observe a stranger about the grounds this evening before supper?"

"There was ol' Clem Tarkenton down the lane, repairing the tinwares an' such," Mary said. "But he's never come up near the house afore, on account o' his dogs bein' so sporty after Mrs. Hepple's chickens."

"I see. Thank you, Mary. And you as well, Thomas. You may go."

For a few seconds he idly rubbed one thumb against the seal on Beecham's note. Then, abruptly, he broke it.

Hallie watched him as he read, watched the lowering of his dark brows and the part to his lips, as though he would read the contents aloud. She silently repeated the words to herself. When at last he looked across at her she felt the intensity in his gaze.

"The poor fool is in love," he said. His eyes, holding hers, were accusing.

"Pardon?"

"Beecham. 'Tis plain as day. The poem says it all. No wonder I have had nothing from him. The besotted moonling has succumbed to the charms of some female. Although," and he frowned, "there is that about it—"

As he returned to the letter, Hallie again rose uncomfortably to her feet and stood with hands clasped before her. She felt cold, miserably cold and utterly unprepared. It was time for the masquerade to end. Jeremy had ensured it. But first she had to ask: "Is it not a good poem?"

"Oh, aye," Marksley muttered as he read. " 'Tis a good and terrible poem."

Hallie swallowed.

"Richard," she began once more, only to falter as that considering gaze suddenly fixed on hers. "There is something I must tell you. I should never have left it so late, but I feared . . . feared you would not understand or . . . forgive." As Marksley's frown deepened, Hallie tried to rush ahead. "Because of my uncle, whom you have reason to know too well, after Tolly's death, I needed a way—" She stopped as a flurry of footsteps in the hall preceded Gibbs and a strange child, an unkempt boy with unruly black hair and ragged clothes that bespoke his gypsy ties. He was very thin, but Hallie guessed him to be about ten years old.

"My lord, this scamp has news of Beecham," Gibbs announced, maintaining a hold on the child's arm, though the boy made no effort to escape.

"Beecham again? Release him then, Gibbs, as I can only assume he came here freely."

"Too right, yer excellency," the boy said in a high treble. " 'At I did. There's a cov what's hurt hisself at our camp, see. An' as none of us knows 'is name—not 'is proper name as you'd know it—there's on'y this then." He handed over a sheet of paper, which Hallie recognized as one of Marksley's letters to Beecham. She had last seen that page when she entrusted it to Jeremy, with the letters of credit for George Partridge.

"George—" she gasped, only to draw her husband's alert regard.

"George?" he asked.

"I . . . it simply reminded me of something. Pardon me."

He looked most dissatisfied, but turned to the boy. "You say the man is injured at your camp?"

"Just happen he stood too close to a fight twixt my uncle Sherengo and Rosabelle's new beau. Hurt 'is head an' arm. 'Taint so bad, but he'd best leave."

"And where are your wagons?"

" 'Bout three miles t'other side o' the river bridge, on the highway. I ken take ya. I ran most the way," he added proudly.

Marksley turned to Gibbs. "I shall take the boy with me on Apollo, Gibbs. Send the carriage after us and summon the doctor. If Beecham can be moved, I shall bring him back here."

"Yes, my lord." Gibbs responded with surprising alacrity, but paused at the door. "This explains the other letter then, my lord, does it not?" To Hallie's hearing, the elderly man sounded relieved.

"It might, Gibbs. It very well might." But Marksley's face was troubled as he at last set Beecham's poem carefully down on his desk. He looked at the boy.

"This stranger . . . he was not your Rosabelle's new beau by any chance?"

"Cor!" The boy exclaimed. "Why Rosabelle wouldna look at him! A *gorgio*—not a brother—an' on'y along to listen to the jib."

"The jib?"

The lad shifted his feet and looked down. "The way we talk 'mong ourselves."

"Will you be afraid to ride with me on my stallion? I shall keep you safe, but he is very tall and fast."

The imp grinned in delight. " 'Taint scared, yer worship," he breathed.

Hallie's thoughts were racing. She felt responsible for George, though she knew he had always pursued his researches in his own eccentric way. That particular note, in which Marksley had explained how the letters of credit would work at the banks, might have led the gypsies to believe he had funds on him or easy access to funds. Why else had the lad been sent all this way, if George's injuries were not severe? Marksley might be heading into a trap.

"My lord," she said, "had you not best take Thomas with you, or perhaps a groom, in case there are many of them?"

Marksley's understanding was quick, but he responded with equanimity. "I am quite certain there are many of them." He turned to the boy. "What did you think when you first read this letter?" he asked.

"Can't read, yer excellency." The boy grinned. "No one can. 'Twas on'y my uncle Sherengo seen the sign," he pointed to the letterhead, "on the gate, out at the road." For a second he looked suspicious. "It's the same sign, idnit?"

As Marksley glanced triumphantly in her direction, Hallie struggled to think of some other way to keep him from the camp. George Partridge had been injured, even if unintentionally. Something similar might happen to Marksley.

"Richard," she urged, surprised by the panic in her voice, "will you not wait for others? Surely the magistrate, Squire Lawes—"

"'Twill be sufficient to inform him once I have assured myself of Beecham's safety." Marksley spoke even as he walked to the door with one hand on the boy's shoulder. He turned to offer her a quick smile. "Do not fret, my dear. I thought you had expressed an interest in this very camp? I promise you I shall return shortly."

She could not believe him. The second he quitted the room, Hallie followed him to the stable, intent on keeping him in view. Perhaps George's injuries were worse than portrayed, enough so that the gypsies had sought outside help. Could not something similar happen to Marksley? That people should settle their differences in so violent a manner led her to suspect the possibility of further harm. In that, she knew, she was interpreting the gypsies' behavior in the worst light, but as all she now cared for rode untroubled into their camp, she could not view the situation dispassionately. Augusta Lawes' dire warnings of their unruly ways had found a susceptible mark after all.

Hallie was determined that Marksley and George should have her aid, that they should not be alone.

She listened to Marksley speaking softly to the restless Apollo as the stallion was saddled. As soon as he had left she presented herself to the stable boy and asked for a mount of her own. The lad looked uneasy; he wished his lady would go out with the carriage, but he did as she requested and dubiously handed her a small lamp as well. Though the night was moonlit and clear, Hallie would be traveling an unfamiliar road and she could not be certain to keep the speedy Apollo in view ahead of her.

Her gentle mare started at a steady trot, leaving Archers' grounds then turning from the road that lead to Penham. In the moonlight, Hallie had no difficulty following the stable boy's direction to the ancient stone bridge over the river. Away from the river the road led to Denhurst and the few lights she could see, but the moonlight, though not full, was sufficient for her needs. Her one challenge was the chill in the air, for though she had draped a wool stable blanket across her shawl, she felt the want of a cloak. Her thin dinner gown hardly sufficed for an autumn night's venture.

When she caught sight of a rider ahead on the road, she quickly doused her light and pressed on. As her mare tossed her head, Hallie concentrated on keeping the animal quiet. The unexpected outing, or perhaps the scent of another horse on the road ahead of them, had clearly excited her.

For a mile or more, the road was level and empty, then it turned away from the river valley and Denhurst, and narrowing, began a gradual, curving ascent through a fragrant forest. The shadows of the trees loomed somberly along the way. Just as the dark proximity of the woods began to oppress her, the trees yielded abruptly to a wide field, lying fallow now in the late season. At the far end, a number of lanterns danced brightly. Though still almost half a mile away, Hallie could hear laughter and smell wood smoke.

Apollo's large, burdened shape was very clear against the lights—too clear, in Hallie's estimation. She dismounted at the lane's margin, leaving the little mare's reins to trail and keep her from wandering, then set out on foot to the gypsy camp.

In the short time it took her to reach the edge of the camp, Hallie's feet in their evening slippers learned to resent the cold, hard ground. She was so chilled that she gazed longingly at the blazing fires around which the caravan clustered. In the flickering firelight, she could see horses and donkeys confined in a makeshift pen of rope and wagons. Dark women in colorful skirts passed to and fro before the flames while children scampered at their feet. A number of scruffy dogs, hungering for scraps from the table, circled a seated group of men. Some raucous game or gambling appeared to be in progress. Occasionally a voice rose above the others or someone laughed loudly.

Hallie's anxious gaze scanned the circle once more. She saw no sign of Marksley, although one of the boys, hovering eagerly near the group of men, looked very much like the young visitor to Archers. Hallie studied the wagons more closely, perceiving that a few of them were occupied, the lamps inside casting silhouettes against curtained windows and entrances.

With deliberation, she moved toward the one closest

to her, prepared to discover Marksley and George Partridge imprisoned inside. But as she neared it, a gypsy woman cradling a baby in her arms stepped forward to the bench seat. Hallie could see that the interior of the wagon did not shelter any other occupants. As the woman cooed softly to the child and started to sing, Hallie slipped away in the wagon's shadow, toward the next. A dog began to bark. For a few seconds Hallie froze, thinking it must have seen her or heard the rustling of leaves as she walked. But the animal was quickly silenced and she carefully moved on.

Before the lamp in the next wagon, two elderly men hunched over a checkerboard. The scent of their pipe smoke hung pleasantly in the air. As Hallie backed away, she reflected that none of the activities in the camp struck her as suspicious in any way. Indeed, given the humble circumstances of its inhabitants, she had increasing doubts. Augusta Lawes' charges against them seemed most implausible. She felt very much the intruder here in this picturesque little community. These people were harmless—they may even have aided a friend. She could see no evidence of any dispute, of the recent fisticuffs that had injured George.

A burst of laughter from the men at their play temporarily halted her steps, but as one of them left the group to take up a fiddle, the music offered a welcome distraction. The haunting strains of the violin mingled with the fires and moonlight in intoxicating combination. For a moment Hallie paused, her senses unexpectedly alive. But she was close to the last wagon.

As she peered in the open back, she saw George Partridge resting in the lamplight, a dirty cloth tied about his balding head and one arm bound in a makeshift sling. His spectacles were askew upon his thin nose, but his eyes were open and bright as he watched Marksley kneeling to blanket him with a heavy traveling cloak.

"I should never have guessed, Partridge," Richard was saying with some amusement, "that you were capable of such adventures. Though I suppose, in the role of Beecham—"

The casualty smiled wanly as Richard reached to straighten his spectacles for him. But George's eyes widened in surprise when he caught sight of Hallie at the entrance.

"I never thought . . . to see you two . . . together," he managed faintly.

Even as Richard spun around, Hallie heard a step behind her.

"*Gorgio shunella*!" a high voice shrieked and bony fingers clutched at her blanket. She heard Richard's sharp "No!" before something struck her.

Chapter Ten

Richard repeatedly relived the events of that night: the lunge to catch Hallie as she fell, the dismay of the gypsy granny who had coshed a slight female instead of a looming, blanketed "listener," the endless, panicked wait for the carriage, the mad dash at midnight back to Archers and the doctor. Two invalids at once were almost more than that poor physician could handle. George Partridge, who had indeed merely witnessed a battle between Romeos, had been promptly patched up and sent along to London the next morning. But now, even after another full day, Hallie still lay in this unmoving state. The cold night air and resulting fever had felled her as surely as that ill-judged blow to the head.

Richard had remained sleepless. Even the long-sought discovery of Henry Beecham's identity had not eased his mind.

Oh, George Partridge had admitted to nothing. And he had said almost as little. Despite holding Beecham's letters, the linguist had been even more taciturn than usual. When taxed about his role as the secretive poet, he had silently demurred, shaking his head and expressing only sincere concern for Hallie's health.

Richard had not pressed him, for George had been nursing a sprained wrist and a devil of a headache, and his concern for Hallie had been justified. Yet there was no recourse beyond patience. So Richard could only sit, powerless, at her bedside. He knew he must leave her shortly to the careful ministrations of Mrs. Hepple and the maids. But her sweet, still features and her lustrous hair, spread against the pillow, kept him watchfully present.

He had been callous and ungracious, only to discover with each passing day how sensitive and honest she was. He would find some way to make amends for all the indignities she had suffered at the hands of the Marksley family—at *his* hands.

He ran a weary palm over his whiskered cheeks. He might start by ridding himself of his beard, lest Hallie wake and quail at the sight of him. At least the task would move him to concentrate on preparing for her return to this world, rather than her demise. That possibility did not bear thought.

He lowered both booted feet to the floor, but as he rose to leave his tired gaze fell upon the journal she kept at her bedside.

He had noticed the familiar volume throughout the

doctor's visits and the careful attentions of the household staff, but he had been too distraught to focus upon it. In any event, he had never been alone. He had not been tempted. Now he was both.

He reached for the book and stood by the bed, at first only admiring the neat hand in the candlelight, thinking that the script suited her. But something about it invited more than passing interest.

The first dated entry was from almost five months before, so she had written a considerable amount. It was a fat volume, with several loose pages tucked among the bindings. He smiled for a moment, remembering her excessive desire the other day to have the journal returned to her care. Young people, he reflected, were possessive of their secrets, so predictably self-conscious. Once he started to read, however, such thoughts fled his mind.

He read rapidly, hungrily, silently repeating certain lines and phrases, noting the fragments of poetry spilled upon the pages like so many gems from a treasure chest—glittering in their own right yet swamped by dazzling company. Though he stood motionless, fixed fast in the candle's flickering light, his pulse increased and the room warmed.

"The little minx—" he muttered and spared one glance at the author, who slept blissfully on.

He held in his hands Henry Beecham, the work so unquestionably the poet's that Beecham might have stamped his signature upon each page. Here was the close attention of the naturalist, recording with an artist's eye the finest raptures of the seasons and the senses. Here was the reflective observer: in spirit with friendship, death, liberty—and love. As with anything Richard had ever read of Beecham's, the words mirrored his own memories and thoughts had he been gifted enough to express them so.

Here too, were a few thumbnail sketches, of flowers, a squirrel, a peddler's cart. One of Jeremy granted him a butterfly's wings. A few small, strong lines rendered Archers's distinctive façade.

There were no references to Richard Marksley.

With growing tension he skimmed the pages, identifying the first stirrings of a poem *The Tantalus* had recently published, noting the dearth of entries for much of the past few weeks, following with fascination how the latest passionate poem had reached fruition. She had taken such care with her script in anything she had sent to him, but she could hide nothing here. Beecham's voice seemed to speak aloud in the quiet predawn darkness.

Why had she not told him? Revealed herself to him at once? Saved herself from his initial disdain, this rudely abrupt marriage—from *him*?

Hallie Ashton, *Henry Beecham,* could only feel trapped by all of this. Richard would have sacrificed much to spare her, to free her from her boorish uncle. He would have paid out a small fortune, even mortgaged Penham, to send her far from any distress.

As his fingers trembled over the pages, three letters fell out upon the floor: two from Jeremy and one of his own. He quickly scanned them, then placed them back in the book. His disappointment was severe; in Jeremy, who had not trusted their friendship; in George Partridge, who had maintained his stoic silence, even yesterday, in the face of all attempts to elicit more from him as 'Beecham;' and in himself, for believing that he and a faceless poet had established a rapport. Why had he not been privy to the secret she shared with Jeremy and George? Perhaps it was understandable that they had remained mum with him; they had respected her wishes, the wishes of an orphaned young woman with little protection and no independent means. But surely *he* had earned her trust as well.

Given the volume's revelations, his own last letter struck him as naïve and misguided. Henry Beecham, *Hallie Ashton*, had simply used him. What did she care for loyalty or sentiment? She did not need encouragement. She had even pulled Jeremy and George into her elaborately constructed web, all to obtain the payments from *The Tantalus*.

He glanced at Hallie's face as he quietly replaced the journal by her bedside. Then, he crossed purposefully to the small desk in her room and searched it. In one of the neatly organized drawers he found a wad of ten pound notes. He could only assume she had troubled to obtain it now in order to flee, to flee *him*. But he was not such a monster! He left the bills in their hiding place, then returned to stand by the window. He reflected moodily on his wife's secret, even as his gaze sought her face anxiously and often.

He should have known her immediately. He should have recognized in her that same rare quality to which he had responded in Henry Beecham, that quality that must have been her soul. He should have recognized her poet's voice. Indeed, he *had* recognized her voice and been enchanted each time she revealed it.

But there was that face. And that decidedly feminine shape. He glanced again at her sleeping form. He could not have reasonably ignored what she could not hide.

Certain mysteries still puzzled him. That last poem had not been the careless jotting of a moment; she had labored over it. The timing led him to think she actually might have cared for Reggie, that those elated, strangely poignant lines were a final dedication to lost love. That thought was troubling enough—so was the possibility that her sense of loss was for Jeremy. She clearly had the warmest sentiments for him, and he for her, else why would he have gone haring off after George during the height of hunting season? Jeremy had been shocked by their speedy marriage. Perhaps the two of them had understood each other too late, else they might have been long gone by now. Yet the dedicated effort to collect Beecham's funds was baffling; Jeremy was one of the wealthiest of the wealthy.

There was a very real likelihood of someone else, someone she had kept as hidden from him and from her uncle as she had hidden her own poetic life. He would not have believed such deception possible—had she not proved it.

He frowned as he watched a soft, gray light fill the

courtyard below, a promising gray like his wife's beautiful eyes. He was amazed she had managed to look at him, to speak to him all these weeks! No woman could be trusted. How artful she had been, even in pseudonym: Harriet Ashton . . . Henry Beecham. *Harvey Oakleigh,* he embellished silently, *Hayes Birchmere, or perhaps even Horatio Larchmont.*

The smile came unbidden, forcing him to acknowledge his reluctant respect for her. She had played a clever game, right under his far too superior nose. Would he not have attempted as much, had his talent been as great, had the constraints of family and position proved as severe? In all honesty, she had, as Henry Beecham, given him months of pleasure. In the person of Hallie Ashton, she had tantalized him daily. He had admitted as much when he had pressed ahead with marriage. He had wanted her and had known he wanted her. He had taken what he wanted.

Yet he could not keep her—that was without question. Henry Beecham's spirit was not one to be imprisoned. And she was in love. The poem had said as much. Though a fierce jealousy pierced him, he knew he must release her. But he would see her safe; she would not be running off alone in the middle of the night.

His gaze traced the smooth curve of her forehead, one delicately arched brow, the full, gently parted lips. She enchanted him. He adored her. Yet, though he loved the woman and the poet, his honor demanded some small recompense. He prayed that she would wake, that those wide eyes would meet his again in full awareness. Only then would he apply her own artful methods, to compel her to explain.

Hallie woke to gaze blankly at Marksley, standing near the foot of her bed, just where the duvet edged the darkness. He faced the window, and the faintest watery light distinguished his profile. His jaw was obstinately set, as though he were angry.

She tried to say his name, but her voice rasped painfully in her dry throat. Still he heard her, for he instantly turned. He poured her a glass of water before coming to sit on the side of the bed.

"Careful now," he said softly, sliding a warm hand gently behind her shoulders and raising her just enough to let her drink.

Hallie closed her eyes as she swallowed gratefully. When she opened them again she read something in his dark eyes that mystified her. Despite the relief he so clearly felt, some other emotion warmed his gaze—some keenness or passion that disconcerted her.

As he lowered her shoulders again to the pillow, which he supported with others, she raised one hand to brush the hair from her forehead. But he captured her fingers and surprised her by planting the softest of kisses upon her palm. The touch made her whole arm tingle.

"What on earth were you thinking," he asked softly, "to waltz into a gypsy camp unannounced?"

"I was . . . worried. About you," she said simply, disarmed by pain and his closeness.

"Me?" The single word seemed to scoff. To Hallie's

sensitive ears, it was too harsh. "Why would you have worried about me?" he asked.

His skepticism tamped her impulse to intimacy and stopped her from admitting more.

"I . . . can't think." She moved her free hand to her throbbing forehead. "If my head is any measure, I shall have difficulty thinking in future."

"The doctor will be in this morning. He'll be delighted, as am I, at your return to us. And there must be something in his magician's bag for the pain."

He still held her hand.

"You were . . . seeing to George?" she asked.

"Yes." With a light kiss to her fingers, Marksley placed her hand on the blanket and sat back. His regard was speculative. Hallie noticed absently that he appeared disheveled, but his tousled hair, shadow of a beard and open throat were not unattractive. He looked as he had the first morning she met him.

She wished her head did not hurt so.

"George Partridge is Henry Beecham, my dear," he told her. "I should have guessed. All the signs were there, had I been alive to them. I already know the man better than I might have anticipated. We had a good laugh over it all as the doctor patched him up." Marksley actually dared laugh again. "George was well enough to return to London yesterday. I have pressed him to help with *The Tantalus*."

Hallie's head refused to clear. A good laugh? *George* as Henry Beecham? She frowned. She had to recall—Marksley had never told her Beecham was a stranger.

"I did not know . . . you had never met Beecham."

"Had I forgotten to tell you that? How odd." His gaze held hers. "Beecham's identity has tormented me for more than a year. But you must have been aware of his secret, for you called him 'George' just now and that night in the library. Do you not remember?"

She tried to swallow.

"How do you know George?" he asked very low.

"He was . . . a friend of my father's."

"Ah! I see. So he had you sworn to secrecy. I presume you placed the poem in the drawing room Saturday night."

She could not meet his gaze. "How long . . . have I been here?" she asked.

"More hours than I care to count. At least a day and a night. 'Tis Monday. The whole household has been eagerly awaiting your recovery. In fact, if I am not very much mistaken, I hear Mary and Mrs. Hepple on the stair." He rose from the bed, leaving Hallie suddenly bereft.

"What hit me?"

"A frying pan, my dear. Wielded by an expert."

"And the gypsies?"

"Gone early the next morning. I am sorry, for they helped George. 'Tis their nature to flee any possibility of trouble with the law, though it was an understandable mistake. Against the light, wrapped in a blanket, peering in upon us in her wagon, you must have looked threatening. She could not tell you were a woman."

"*She?*"

Marksley grinned.

"An octogenarian grandmother, their most convincing fortune teller. *Un*fortunately, she could not see your palm." He smiled. "You see why I've not informed Squire Lawes of your injury. Though of course, if you should prefer—"

"No, no. I must have frightened her."

"All the same," and his voice took on a sharper edge, "She had surprising strength. She might have killed you, my dear. I regret that I was moved to confiscate her weapon."

Sensing his resolve even as he stood there by her bed, Hallie could well imagine how inflexibly tough he might have been with anyone else.

"What a . . . boisterous evening, to be sure," she managed, earning another laugh and, astonishingly, a quick, cool kiss against her pounding forehead.

Mrs. Hepple and Mary beamed as they noticed Marksley pulling away from her. They made much of her recovery and offered to bring her anything she might want.

Hallie glanced at Marksley as he observed them. *If you would just keep kissing me,* she implored him silently, *I would need nothing more.* But he kept his distance from their bustle and excused himself when the women proposed to help her bathe.

Hallie submitted to their care and listened with strained attention to Mrs. Hepple's chatter regarding the events of the past two days. She mentioned that

"Mr. Partridge" had stayed only through the previous morning and that he had left them well fed and with only a sprained wrist, not a broken arm. Hallie knew she must write to him. George had kept her secret, even when confronted with Marksley's false conclusion regarding Beecham. George had been a most loyal friend, yet she had not thanked him even for his help in obtaining her funds.

Hallie's anxiety regarding George grew so great that when she returned to bed she requested some writing paper. Despite a maddening weakness in her fingers, which made positioning the pen and paper difficult, Hallie expressed her gratitude for George's help, her apologies for drawing him away from his studies, and her heartfelt wishes for his quick recovery. She would, she claimed, soon straighten out the Beecham matter.

As soon as the page was dry she leaned back, exhausted, and contemplated the shadows on the plastered ceiling.

George as Henry Beecham. It made so much sense. George was everything Marksley would believe as Beecham: learned, observant, sensitive . . . male. And during her illness, George had somehow managed to convince Marksley. Or Marksley had simply assumed.

George was so very quiet. If he were to have infrequent contact with Marksley in the future, perhaps Hallie could encourage George to continue to pose—

Her hand shook above the letter, leaving an inkblot upon the page.

This must stop, Jeremy had said. The sharp words haunted her.

Not only illness made her weak. She no longer recognized herself. She was so greedy for Richard Marksley's company that she now lacked even courage to leave him, though she at last possessed the means. And as for telling him the truth . . . what had happened to her resolute attempts of the other night? Now she had George Partridge lying for her!

Jeremy might claim she had lost "only" her heart, but she did not like the calculating creature she'd become. She had reasoned that by maintaining Henry Beecham she was preserving something Marksley valued and wanted, perhaps the only thing he wanted from her. But he would also have wanted honesty.

She had not known love could be so selfish. Apparently, she and principle had parted ways.

She was so very tired.

With a sigh, she folded her letter and put aside the pen and writing box.

"Is someit wrong, milady?" Mary asked, coming to remove them.

"I shall have to write more later, Mary. I am too tired now." She rested her head against the pillows. Even that slight pressure revealed the tenderness on her scalp. As soon as she felt well enough, she promised, closing her eyes, she would confess to Richard Marksley. She was tired of subterfuge. She would make no further demands upon him. He had done so very much. . . .

Hallie slept through the remainder of the day, waking only for a light tea and an unexpected visit from her husband. He appeared refreshed and had tidied himself considerably. Once again neatly outfitted, the Viscount Langsford looked infinitely less approachable than he had early that morning. The task of explaining herself to him seemed even more difficult.

"You have a sympathetic crew most concerned about your accident, and most eager to welcome you once again to their company," Marksley told her, walking only to the foot of the bed, where he grasped one of the posts. "Mrs. Lawes and her daughter are tempting us with another invitation to dinner—once you are feeling much better, naturally. The vicar has inquired as to your health, and Mrs. Mayhew sent over her best wildflower honey, which I highly recommend." Again, Hallie remarked the appraisal in his gaze. "I belatedly remembered our friend Jeremy and sent a note along to him at the inn, only to hear that his father called him home yesterday for Rowena's nuptials. Have you met Jeremy's sister? No? Well, it is a growing mystery to me why so many are impulsively marriage-minded these days." Marksley treated her to a self-conscious smile. "Should you wish to send a message, I will most happily forward it."

"Thank you. I have . . . had some difficulty writing."

"Have you? I am sorry to hear it. I know how dedicated you are to your journal entries. Though, when one has been unconscious, one should make allowances—"

He bowed, but his expression was amused. Enough so that Hallie decided he had a low opinion of female scribblings. The thought annoyed her, but she could do little more than glare at him.

"No doubt, my lord, having been favored with the very best in literature, you would find my trivial reflections most tedious."

He surprised her by smiling even more fully.

"I would have no means of judging, my dear, unless you were to permit me to read them." He quit his position to walk around to her side, within a few inches reach of the night table and her journal. Hallie gazed wide-eyed from the book to his pleasantly smiling face. When he moved his hand, as though to reach for her journal, Hallie cringed. But he placed his warm palm against her forehead.

"I am delighted to see you better, Hallie," he said softly and with unexpected sincerity. He only slowly withdrew his hand. "I feared I might lose you."

He held her gaze for a long moment. Confronted with the too-discerning gravity of that look, Hallie glanced down and plucked nervously at the edge of the bed linens.

"Thank you," she replied just as softly. She felt peculiarly enervated, lethargic. She heard his small sigh before he turned to walk to the window. The reflection of lanterns, ablaze along the terrace below, softly highlighted his face.

"Once you are well, Hallie, I should like to hold a gathering—a soiree, if you will—at Penham. To introduce Beecham—" he turned briefly to smile at her frozen features, "George Partridge, that is, to some of my acquaintance. My aunt and uncle depart for Bath on the morrow—the waters promise some relief to the Earl—so the Hall is mine to command. I would make all the arrangements, of course, with the help of Mrs. Hepple and Gibbs. You need not trouble yourself with a thing, apart from continuing to improve apace and wearing your very best frock on the occasion. A tall order, I know, but 'twill not be done without you."

"Does—does George Partridge know?"

"Yes indeed. He is anticipating his introduction, in his persona as a most acclaimed poet, to an eager public."

"Is he? I should think, that having hidden away, having . . . dissembled for so long, he might prefer to remain anonymous."

"Having *dissembled* for so long you think he might wish to continue to *dissemble?*" Marksley's look was daunting. She could not gauge his mood, which had become an obstacle. She focused her attention desperately on the far corner of the room, so that she would not have to face his scrutiny. "Tell me, my dear; since you claim an acquaintance with Mr. Partridge, do you think that very likely?"

"No. But he must have had a very good reason for engaging in the ruse in the first place."

Marksley did not respond immediately. Hallie could feel his attention, like a strangely searching caress, upon her face and nervous fingers.

"He wanted to write popular verse, my dear. Not a pursuit a respected scholar of etymology will embark upon without first testing the waters. Reputations are fragile things."

"I see." But Hallie did not truly see. Had George really fabricated such an intricate explanation? The George Partridge she knew was an unassuming man who could, and would, remain silent for hours at a time. His vocation, after all, was to listen. He might never reveal a secret, but, by the same measure, he was most unlikely to trouble to construct a lie.

"I should not keep you, Hallie, though it pleases me that you appear to be recovering your strength and spirits. Is there anything you need, anything I might bring you?"

Hallie looked at him and almost pleaded, *Stay here with me*. Even the thought brought the blood to her cheeks.

"There," Marksley noted. "You appear to be regaining some of your color. I hope you will be fit enough to join me for a meal tomorrow," he said, even as he moved to the door. "Cook has been most disappointed, having experimented only briefly with menus for newlyweds."

"She must be excited by the prospect of your soiree."

Marksley raised an eyebrow.

"Indeed." And as he bowed and left the room, Hallie thought she heard him mutter, "as are we all."

Chapter Eleven

By the next morning, Hallie could no longer bear the confines of her bedroom. She asked Mary to help her dress. When the maid in turn insisted on accompanying her downstairs to the dining room, Hallie found she could not object. The first sight of the stairs left her feeling more than a little dizzy. But she carefully negotiated her way to the hall, only to be told by Gibbs that Marksley had already breakfasted and left on Apollo to visit tenants.

"I had wanted to join him, Gibbs," she said.

"Yes, my lady. Perhaps once you are well."

"But I am well. As you see, I . . . Thank you, Gibbs."

She would have to do something immediately about this perception that she was little more than an invalid. But much as she wished to stride confidently into breakfast, her legs intended her to do something else altogether. Hallie reached a chair and gratefully grasped the back, only to notice at least three hovering, concerned faces. Her husband must have set the whole household to watching her.

"I am quite all right. Please carry on," she told them, even as she dropped into her seat.

Beside her place Marksley had left a stack of papers, which she recognized as her own. *These are Beecham's,* he had written. *I thought you might like to review them before our soiree.*

Hallie glanced at the neatly ordered pages. She felt the suggestion as a rebuke. That their correspondence had come to this! She had trapped herself in her own creation. And she could not review the sheets. She knew their lying contents by heart.

She was not left to herself for the rest of the day. She managed to win ten minutes on the terrace only by consenting to dress as though for a blizzard, and, as she walked slowly across the worn brick, she could see someone at the door every time she glanced toward the house. Hallie pointedly kept her gaze on the garden.

Winter, in its impatience, had sighed upon the trees and flowerbeds. The lingering warmth and color of three days before had fled even from the late blooming asters, and though the beeches hoarded their faded copper foliage, many other trees had lost their leaves. In the slightest of breezes, those still clinging to branches voiced a rustling protest.

Hallie had always loved autumn with its preparation

and tranquil progression. But this year the season's melancholy affected her adversely. She had loved fall when she had supposed spring, and now she would not be continuing as she had been. Her life as a poet, whether Henry Beecham were revealed or not, would never be the same. She must say goodbye to the ways that had sustained her, with no assurance of what was to follow. And even though she might perform as she ought, act as she ought, her heart was not ready for bold new adventures.

'Love is a durable fire,' she recalled, and sought solace in Marksley's library. The volumes contained wisdom and direction, but could not serve as her proxies.

Marksley did not return in time to join her for dinner.

"He's up at the Hall," Mrs. Hepple told her, "making arrangements." She frowned. "Though 'tis not like the master—Lord Langsford—to keep his doings so close. The housekeeper as is over there told Pickens, that's the head gardener, brother of our Thomas, that though the rooms are being aired, nothing else has been readied."

Hallie, who had no concept of how such a gathering was to be planned, merely shrugged. "Perhaps the Viscount is inviting so many people from London that he has found it necessary to lodge his visitors elsewhere."

Mrs. Hepple shook her head. " 'Twould not be necessary, milady. Not at Penham." She continued to frown. "No invitations have been sent to the post."

That did puzzle Hallie, since Marksley had implied the event would be soon.

"Lord Langsford may be delaying until he feels I am better," she suggested.

Mrs. Hepple's frown fled. "And that does sound just like him, milady. Ever since he was a boy, he was that considerate of others."

He had certainly been considerate of her. How comfortable it would be—how cowardly it would be—simply to let George continue as Beecham, to hide here with Marksley and have him learn to care for her. It was a most seductive thought. But the risk in choosing to do nothing was comparably great. To the extent he cared for her now, he might never care for her again, for no one appreciated being fooled.

She sought relief in sleep, however restless, and in the morning, heavy-eyed, again made her way down to breakfast, this time negotiating the steps with little difficulty. Her body was much improved, yet her mind was far from easy.

She must send her letter to George.

Marksley was seated at the table when she entered the dining room. He rose and bowed as she moved toward him.

"I trust you are feeling much better this morning, Hallie?"

"I am, thank you." For some reason she could not fathom, she vividly recalled how he had slid his arm about her shoulders to give her a drink of water. Coloring, she looked toward the buffet. All she really wanted was another sip of water—served just the same way.

"I should just like some toast this morning please, Gibbs," she said as she walked to a chair. Marksley was there before her, to pull it out for her before Gibbs could reach it. Even having him that close caused her breath to catch in her throat.

As she sat down she sensed him behind her, sensed that he stared at the back of her head, thought that perhaps he even leaned toward her. She could feel his breath tease her hair and willed his lips to seek her nape. He was that close. But he returned to his seat.

"It is no longer the size of a melon," he remarked with satisfaction. He took a sip of tea and watched her face.

"Pray sir," Hallie said, trying to control her unreasoning disappointment. "Which fruit or vegetable does my skull now resemble?"

"Your skull, my dear, is as attractively shaped as a skull may be. I would estimate your injury, however, to be the size of a squashed plum. 'Twas a flat iron pan that hit you, after all. Had your head not been as hard as it has proved to be, you might not have been breakfasting with me now." For a moment, his gaze was very direct and serious.

"I descend from a long line of hard heads, my lord," Hallie offered. "Notorious for their fortitude." *And for their stupidity,* she added silently.

Marksley raised a brow. "I trust the trait has rarely been tested so severely."

"Only in the abstract," she said lightly. For an instant their glances locked, in communication that was strangely paralyzing. Then he turned his attention to the stacked letters at his side.

Hallie drank her tea and listened to the rustling of

pages from Marksley's reading. The silence was companionable enough, yet she found herself waiting for something—something more, certainly, than the plate of toast Gibbs delivered to her.

She set about methodically buttering the hot squares.

Though he held a letter in his hands, Marksley observed the practice, and her, with an amiable smile, before he cleared his throat.

"My dear Beecham—" At once Hallie's knife stilled. "Forgive me, I mean George Partridge—writes that he is looking forward to this evening's event."

"This evening?"

"Yes, I believe we have waited long enough." Marksley placed the letter to the side before looking up at her. "If you are feeling quite the thing?"

"I . . . I am well."

"I see no reason for delay." Marksley sat back in his chair and steepled his hands before him. "Several important guests are housed already at Penham. And many of those who most closely follow *The Tantalus* and literary matters will be leaving London this morning. If you would prefer not to join us tonight, Hallie, there would be opportunity enough over the next two days to make the acquaintance of Beecham's admirers."

"Well, it is a bit sudden—"

"Sudden? I shouldn't think so. The man has been eluding us for more than a year. Hiding and feinting and slipping away. No, the fox has finally been run to ground. And the hounds must have their triumph." He observed Hallie's involuntary wince and smiled encouragement. "Do not worry, my dear. This is his triumph as well. 'Tis his craft everyone would celebrate after all, and our shy versifier willingly agreed to attend."

Marksley picked up the letter he had been reading and waved it at her, as though demonstrating the proof of his words. Hallie wondered how George, even as gifted as he was, had managed to copy her script for an entire letter. But she recalled that he would have had her own letter to use as a model. He *could* have done it, but why would he? She would never have believed him capable of such a ruse, even to protect her interests.

"Have you had a chance . . . to read his work?" Marksley asked.

The soft question pinned her like one of Jeremy's fragile specimens. Her lips parted, but no words came. He seemed so convinced, so content with George as Beecham.

Marksley watched her.

"I see I was too forward in assigning you reading while you are still recovering. But I do hope you will accompany me, my Lady Langsford," Marskley persisted, "or is your frown answer in itself?"

"I fear I have nothing appropriate to wear to so grand an occasion."

"Nonsense. I have seen to it that the dress you selected for our wedding has been finished just as you chose. Would you not appreciate the opportunity to wear it? I should like to see you in it."

"But . . . we are in mourning—"

"You are still a bride."

Hallie could not look him in the eye. "I have no experience . . . London society is—"

"No worse than one of Augusta Lawes's suppers," he said, then sighed. "Granted, that can be trying enough, but you have proved yourself more than capable." He fixed her with an inquiring gaze. "Would you not like to see Beecham, your friend George, again?"

"Will he not stay with us?"

For a moment, Marksley looked uncertain. "I have hopes he might. But it seems unlikely. He has made no promises."

No promises! She had made bold promises indeed. But she was promising to break them.

"You are frowning again, Hallie. Have you . . . something to say?"

Her imagination lent urgency to his tone.

"I . . . should like to join you this evening."

"Splendid," he said, though his smile seemed forced. "I am delighted. 'Twould be nothing without you, my dear. Although I recommend you rest this afternoon." He rose from the table and gathered his correspondence. "Please excuse me for now. Perhaps I shall see you for tea later?"

He paused by her chair and took her right hand in his. His warm palm swallowed her fingers as he raised them to his lips. Only the faintest caress skimmed her knuckles, but it was enough to make her tremble.

She sat very still for a minute after he had left. Her tea cooled, her toast cooled, but her mind and heart were afire. And Marksley, for all his civility and excuses regarding his pressing correspondence, was clearly avoiding her. She was not imagining his distance. Why was he now so impatient of her company? It had been easier to understand his disdain.

She had wondered if he might learn to love her, if she might build upon the same qualities of empathy and understanding that had sustained their correspondence. But now, it seemed, something about her person was not to his liking.

He did not join her at all during the day, and Hallie was too embarrassed to ask Gibbs where her husband might be. She spent the time in her rooms, submitting to a last fitting of her dress and sleeping when she could no longer read. By four, when she had a light tea, preparatory to bathing and dressing, she was both more rested and more anxious. The evening promised to be awkward, to say the least. She would have to find and speak to George before Marksley made any announcement. And even at this late hour she had not decided what to say or to whom. They might all assume her head injury had caused delusions.

Tolly would have been ashamed of her.

Mary enthused over the dress, a gossamer creation of ivory silk and lace. Mrs. Hepple smiled her approval, even Gibbs granted Hallie a grin as she entered the front hall. Only her husband surveyed her with apparent indifference.

"Suits you then, does it?" he asked at last.

"As you see, my lord. 'Tis hardly sackcloth."

"True enough. Though you would grace even sackcloth, my lady. Shall we go?"

As discomposed by the compliment as by its earlier absence, Hallie nodded her agreement and took his arm. Outside, the groom held the horses harnessed to the Penham carriage. The driver gaily tipped his hat to her.

Marksley helped her to a seat, covered her lap with a blanket, then took the bench opposite. He tapped the roof of the carriage. With an easy, concerted surge the horses pulled forward.

They traveled in silence through the dusk. With occasional glances Hallie observed Marksley's fine formal clothing, the thoughtful set of his features. Tonight, she imagined, he himself might have been called "The Gorgeous Langsford." But after some time, she determined he did not look excited.

"You do not appear to be anticipating this . . . Richard." When he glanced rather sharply at her she wondered why the observation annoyed him. "Or perhaps I assume too much."

"No, you are quite correct." The attempt at a smile made his too serious demeanor all that much more noticeable. "I am not anticipating much of anything. The discovery has been made, has it not?" As Hallie shrank a bit into her corner, he added, "This evening is a beginning, certainly. For Beecham and, perhaps, for myself. Yet, in the best poetic tradition, I am aware as well of what is ending."

She considered his words as she glanced out the window at the deepening darkness. The bare branches of trees were stark against the sky.

"In each moment the moment past," she agreed softly. At his silence she turned to meet his stare. His expression was most peculiar. In the dim light, he looked as though he were in pain.

"Richard," she leaned towards him, "what is wrong?"

The carriage lurched, propelling her forward against the squabs. She felt for a second as though her neck had snapped from her shoulders. As she collected her wits, she realized Marksley had grasped her arms and still held her firmly.

"Are you injured?" he asked quickly.

When she shook her head, he released her to rap sharply on the carriage roof. "Peters, whatever is the matter?"

"Lamed, he is, my lord," came the gruff reply from the front. "Must be a stone. Pulled up right sudden." The carriage rocked gently as Peters climbed down.

"Pardon me, my dear." Marksley rose to follow the driver to the ground. Hallie heard a few angry words, then the murmur of conversation and the sound of horses being released from their harnesses. Marksley came back to look at her through the open door.

"Peters will ride back for another leader," he told her, "but I fear we will be delayed here for a little while. We have the good fortune, however, of being only a few steps from Haskell's mill."

Hallie, glancing quickly at her beautiful new gown, hesitated to test it in the neglected building.

"The mill is . . . rather dusty, Richard—"

"No longer. After finding it in such a sorry state, I ordered it cleaned and repaired. Come . . . help me inspect it."

He lifted her lightly from the carriage, then collected one of the lanterns from the side of the door. Hallie stepped carefully beside him. Her soft slippers had been fashioned for ballrooms, not country walks. The path was uneven, littered with small stones. But once they reached the door to the mill she noticed immediately the improvements Marksley had claimed. The floor had been swept and scrubbed, shutters hung true on their hinges, a glazier had carefully replaced every broken pane. No sign of a cobweb was to be seen. Oddly, a fire blazed at the front parlor's wide stone hearth.

"You are as good as your word, my lord. You have set the place to rights. You might almost host your elegant soiree in such a spot."

"How curious that you should think so." Marksley moved closer to her and reached to light another lantern on the table. "Most curious indeed. Because I intend to do just that."

Until that moment, it had not occurred to her that Haskell's mill was not on the road to Penham. As she looked her bewilderment, he smiled, but did not explain.

"Puzzling, is it not?" he asked instead. "I seem to have devilishly bad luck on this stretch of road."

"It is . . . simply coincidence." Hallie found it difficult not to stare at him, he looked so very handsome in the warm lamplight. And she recalled too vividly what had almost happened at the mill.

"I believe you will find the place comfortable enough now, my dear, which will suit my purposes admirably. We have some weighty matters to discuss."

"But your plans for the evening. We are expected—"

"I expect only one person, and he," Marksley's glance moved beyond her to the front door, "is here. Welcome, Henry Beecham," he said with a smile. "Do come meet my wife." And Hallie wheeled to face the entrance.

Chapter Twelve

Even as she swayed, Marksley clasped her shoulders, holding her loosely but securely from behind.

"Yes, Harriet Ashton *Marksley.*" The urgent words tickled her cheek. "You of the dove-gray eyes and capricious butterflies. This must end." His fingers tightened briefly before he released her.

Hallie turned slowly to face him. She could still sense his touch, though he had no hold upon her.

"How long have you known?" she asked.

"Since your illness."

"George Partridge told you?"

"George said nothing. I . . . read your journal." At her gasp, he opened his palms to her. "An unforgivable act, granted," he said, "but I was beyond patience. You must admit your own trespasses are considerable. And

I would have my little revenge. It may gratify you to know, though, how very empty it feels."

"There is no soiree," she said slowly, reading his gaze. "There are no guests from London." When Marksley could not stop a small smile, she dared to feel angry. "Why here?" She indicated the empty room.

"I have fond memories of the place." He glanced briefly at her lips, then leaned closer. "And *you* chose to leave this matter so late. Here there will be no interruptions. No gypsy boys, no lepidopterists, no bullying uncles, or insufferable Archies. No acts, I pray, of God." He added softly, "My dear Beecham, your little game is over."

"'Twas never a game, my lord. 'Twas life for me. And I never meant for it to continue this long."

"You are not helpless, Hallie. You might have told me at any time."

"I did try."

"And what prevented you?"

Her lips rose. "Gypsy boys, insufferable Archies—" But he was not smiling back at her. "I see I must tell you the whole."

"I would be most grateful." The comment was in the nature of a plea.

She turned from his too-open gaze.

"I . . . have told you about my cousin, about Tolliver. He was a dear brother to me, like a family in just the one. Tolly had always enjoyed my 'verses' as he called them; he wrote me from the Peninsula that he had even read some to his company. He claimed they were much appreciated, but I thought little of it until after—until after he died.

"Jeremy was with Tolly in France, and he sought me out afterward to tell me . . . about how it had happened. About those last days. I needed to know. He had heard Tolly read from my letters. Jeremy witnessed my circumstances with uncle and he wanted to help. He encouraged me to submit my poems to *The Tantalus,* suggesting you would be pleased to publish them. Jeremy said . . . you would consider only the quality of the poems."

"Yes," Marksley agreed, in such a tone that Hallie's attention shot to his face.

"'Twas not Jeremy's idea for me to assume the pen name. He was a fair friend and argued that you would not balk at publishing a woman."

"Bravo, Jeremy," Marksley muttered. "Yet he honored your desire in the matter. I believe I shall have much to say to him when next we meet. But do go on."

Hallie swallowed.

"Well . . . you know my uncle and Millicent. I feared my uncle's temper. I had no one else—my father died when I was fourteen—and no resources. The small legacy due to me will not be mine until next year. You have not read all my journals, my lord. You cannot know how difficult it was for me. The poems were relief, yes, they gave me purpose, but 'twas like speaking into a gale. Someone stronger, or perhaps with less to say, might have remained quiet. But I—" She drew a breath. "Jeremy trusted you would publish, but I did not know you, so I dared not trust you. It was too important to me to have someone listen. I am still not certain that you would have published a woman's poems."

"I *have* published a woman's poems."

"But you did not know she was a woman."

"Unfortunately not." He smiled, which she found she could not abide.

"Sir," she said sharply, "you cannot lie to me."

"No, my dear, I am quite certain I cannot. Or not nearly as well as you can lie to me." He knew that had hurt her, because he turned away. "Still . . . I would like to believe that I'd have found a way. If not perhaps in *The Tantalus*, then in a separate—"

"Precisely, my lord. In something separate and quite, quite apart. In one of the publications for ladies—those that are scarcely read and so easily disdained even before reading. If you deemed such sufficient, my lord, why do you not pen *The Tantalus* for the ladies?"

"I might yet, my dear. Now that I know there is so much talent to be had." His glance was amused and something else she could not identify. Could he have been proud of her? As her confidence faltered she glanced down. She was conscious of the absurdity of debating in this abandoned mill in her wedding gown.

"There were clues," she said, "signs by which you might have known Henry Beecham was a woman."

"Ah, Hallie! Do you truly believe so?" He smiled. "You say there were clues. You see them because you provided them. But try to understand the position of your reader, poor deluded R.E. Marksley. He believes in other clues. He might think he knows his author, that by some experience or insight all is revealed to him. If the writer is good, that is. And when the writer is exceptional—" he stopped, and his gaze sought hers, "as you are, poor Marksley hears himself as well. He says: this writer thinks as I think, feels as I feel." He cleared his throat.

"I know so little of women—" Catching the incredulity in her gaze he amended, "in that respect. How could I have supposed you so different from myself? And someone as young as you are. You are quite correct; I would not have believed it. But that is the irony. I also dared imagine, and imagination is often false to reality. Knowing you now, having seen your journal, all of this seems not only plausible, but right. Do you comprehend, though, how impossible it would have been to deduce? I should set you a challenge, my dear, and have you guess at authorship. I think you would be surprised."

"I did not intend to fool anyone."

"Didn't you?" His smile disputed the claim. "Such elaborate efforts seem calculated to fool *someone*. Permit me to say that you seem confused."

Confused! The word was inadequate.

"Tell me, Hallie," he pursued. "What could have compelled you to find so drastic an undertaking as marriage to a virtual stranger, to *me*, to be preferable to discovery?"

She could hear the edge to his voice. She must have him understand.

"I did try to leave before this eventuality . . . before

our agreement became permanent. If you read my journal, you may have seen the letters?" He nodded. "*The Tantalus*—you, Richard Marksley—had paid me a goodly sum. But Jeremy arrived too late and now . . . I find I cannot."

"No, you certainly cannot," Marksley agreed shortly. "I've been determined to have you speak with me before absconding."

"Absconding!"

"Was that not your plan?"

"I—hardly absconding!"

"Nevertheless." He shrugged. "Pray continue. I find myself intrigued after so many months of correspondence. Correspondence that, by the way, I thought genuine, and that I found eminently satisfactory in its candor and confiding friendship." He held her gaze. "You might have trusted me, Hallie. Or entertained the notion that the rest of us have feelings, though not perhaps as delicately discriminating as your own. Did you not once consider revealing your true identity to me?" he asked bitterly.

"I did," Hallie said, clasping her hands nervously before her. "And I did."

Marksley looked more patient than amused.

"You must explain your riddle, my dear. I find my stumbling mind struggles to your pace."

"Reginald," she said. "'Tis why I confronted your cousin. At the inn at Tewsbury. I heard his two companions speaking with him. He made some quip they found witty and one of them clapped him on the back and claimed it was 'truly worthy of R.E. Marksley.' I did not suspect them of sarcasm. As they were served, I overheard them making a toast 'to literature.' Even then I had no thought to be bold. But we passed in the corridor and I . . . I addressed him as Mr. Marksley, and told him I was a friend of Henry Beecham's. The rest you know."

"No, I do not know," he countered darkly. "He took advantage of you?"

"He pulled me into a side room, asked me how old Beecham was getting on, called me smart and saucy and . . . kissed me. Millicent found us before I could break away. Then he claimed to be Marksley of *The Tantalus*."

Marksley observed her as her hand covered her lips. "I have been apologizing for Reggie for many years," he told her. "It seems I must continue to do so even after his death."

"I was foolish and forward. I have not wanted to admit to you just how foolish I was."

Marksley shook his head and moved as though he would reach for her. But his arm fell away. "How can I fault you," he said softly, "for at last seeking me out? I never thought I would be grateful for Miss Binkin, Hallie, but, in all honesty, she may have spared you much. Reginald was known for worse. We can hardly dispute, though, that the result was as undesirable as anything else that he ever contrived. If you had only turned to me at once—" His glance held hers. "Perhaps your caution was understandable. I have behaved contemptibly. You must lay my bad temper at the door of jealousy."

Jealousy? Of his cousin? Reginald Marksley could never have held a candle to him—surely he must know that.

"I would never have married Reginald Marksley," she told him.

"I am glad to hear it, although I suspect you would have had no more choice in the matter than you had in marrying me. For the past two days, however, I have been very busily engaged in assuring you are not married at all." He turned away from her to watch the river. "In addition to forwarding the funds Beecham earned in all fairness, I have arranged for your passage to Italy. You will, I hope, enjoy my friend's villa in the north, at Lago Maggiore, for however many weeks or months may suit you. An annulment is difficult, but hardly impossible. I have sounded out my solicitor. The process will take some time. Needless to say, he was surprised and concerned." He paused briefly. " 'Twas just last week he was drawing up settlements. But Fulton is discreet. You will be at liberty to write and travel as you choose—as you deserve, Hallie. The thought that a sensibility such as yours should be confined in any manner is abhorrent. Henry Beecham always wrote freely—and of freedom. He might enjoy its experience."

For a moment, Hallie could only study his back—the implacable set of his shoulders in that midnight blue coat. Then he turned to her.

"It is a remedy, of a sort. If after some time you choose to return to England, my expectation would be that any gossip will have run its course. There is a certain relief in how quickly new misfortunes claim the scandalmongers' interest. Then, should you wish to marry Jeremy, you would face no difficulty."

"I do not wish to go to Italy," she said softly.

"Well, perhaps somewhere else then. Jeremy might wish to help you with your plans. Though why he could not simply have given you the funds you needed—"

"I would not have taken money from him. 'Twould not have been proper."

"Less proper than marrying me? I believe I hold the institution of marriage in higher esteem than you do, my dear. Now if *Jeremy* had married you—"

"I would not have married Jeremy. I might have married Jeremy at any time," she told him boldly, "and I did not."

Again, he frowned.

"I have been trying—I have tried to make amends, Hallie. If none of this appeals to you, you must of course let me know. A certain amount of notoriety is inevitable, but those with literary leanings seem to be indulged these days. Conventions need not bind anyone of talent and purpose, particularly with the wherewithal—"

She interrupted him. "You speak of conventions, of how objectionable they can be, and yet you have professed that what might be acceptable to the radicals would not be acceptable to you."

"I do not recall—"

"You said as much to Archie Cavendish . . . and to me."

"There are many things I'd have dearly loved to have said to Mr. Cavendish, Hallie. Yet as I remember that particular interview, I was trying—rather too hard—to feign an indifference I was far from feeling. Your friend Cavendish assumed I must condone certain reckless and dishonorable behaviors. I mustn't, and I do not. I have not," he stressed. "Surely one may speak generally with regard to society's strictures, without advocating their eradication?"

"Then you will understand that I . . . I do not want an annulment."

At that he looked perplexed. Then his gaze narrowed.

"I see. You prefer, after all, to be a viscountess." He shrugged, which incensed her. "Perhaps Fulton can arrange something along those lines. I shall not marry again. My aunt will no doubt find that unacceptably contrary, but I—"

"Oh, will you not listen?" Her own voice startled her even as it silenced him. "You have made every plan, you have been most honorable and generous, yet everything you have said . . . everything you have chosen to interpret—oh, I cannot breathe!" She turned to the windows and spread her fingers against the cold glass panes. The darkness outside reflected her ghostly white form, framed by Marksley's dark shape behind her.

"May I tell you what I wanted?" She spoke to his image in the glass. "All I have ever wanted? I wanted to continue as Henry Beecham, to write to you and have you respond to me, as nobly and kindly and cleverly as you always had. I wanted to save something of that, of what I treated as friendship. And to have you value me, not knowing anything else of me. But I also wanted to sit at breakfast with you and hear you laugh and have you hold my hand. To have you look at me as you do sometimes, even when you are angry. I wanted both. Only everything changed—such that I knew I could not have both. And now I see I shall have neither."

For a moment she heard only her heart, beating too loudly in her ears and in the stillness. Then Marksley asked softly, "That poem—the one you left me the night I set out to find George. The night you braved the gypsy camp. I would have sworn Henry Beecham was in love—with Jeremy Asquith?"

She turned at the question, but hid her trembling hands behind her.

"Would Henry Beecham be in love with Jeremy Asquith?" she asked. She felt at once expectant and afraid.

"Would he?" Some growing comprehension softened Marksley's expression. "When did you write that poem, Hallie?"

"I was writing it at Penham. I finished it at Archers that morning. I wished to say goodbye."

"That was not a farewell," Marksley insisted. "It was a love poem." His steady gaze would not permit her to look away.

She swallowed and raised her chin.

"Perhaps it was, then. Or one of joy. A joy that promised everything in life for the faint favor of my own. I could not . . . I could not refuse it. But it had to be returned, in the only way I knew to return it. In a small, spare sum of words. Yes—if it pleases you," her gaze at last fell to the floor. " 'Twas of love."

In the seconds following, she wondered at the silence. Surely he should laugh, or clear his throat in embarrassment, or storm from the room in disgust? She was too conscious of the warmth in her cheeks and constriction in her chest.

"Do you wish to know my very first thought on seeing you, Hallie," he said at last, so gravely that she was drawn to look up at him, "that astonishing morning at Archers? With your red-faced uncle breathing down my neck, and Miss Binkin and Geneve pushing me at once toward marriage and Bedlam?" While she hungrily watched his face he stepped closer. "I wondered what unintended good I had done in life to deserve even to meet you."

"Then you played . . . as carefully at our contest . . . as I," she managed, "for you gave every indication . . . you despised my company. And after we were wed . . . you could not suffer more than fifteen minutes in my presence."

"My sweet, I could not bear it," he said simply. "What hint had I that you had ever come to me willingly? My harsh treatment had all to do with Reggie and the circumstances, naught to do with my inclinations. And after discovering your secret, I knew that I would have to let you go. The prize seemed always to dance before me, ever out of reach." He captured one of her hands. "Dare I believe that I might make you happy? I find I haven't the heart for anything else."

He drew her arms to his. He kissed her hands and fingers and finally both palms, while she still stood entranced.

"The gypsies read my fortune that night, Hallie, before they took me to see George Partridge. They believe their gift of foresight offers a glimpse at character, into divining one's purpose. Amid much jesting they revealed to me that I would love a man. Needless to say, I was surprised." He drew her a few inches closer and again kissed her trembling fingers.

"And do you," she breathed, " 'love a man?' "

"Aye," he smiled broadly. "Henry Beecham—and his fiendish twin, Harriet."

She knew she returned his smile. Every part of her smiled.

"But if I had . . . if Henry Beecham had been a man?"

He sighed and pulled her abruptly to him.

"Then, dear heart, you may trust I'd have quoted something else at Augusta Lawes' dinner. 'Let me not,' " he spoke to her lips, " 'to the marriage . . . of true minds . . . admit impediments.' "